Unit

J.L. Hart

Special thanks to:
Alaina Whaley
Raistlin Colbert
Maddie Cutrell
Amanda Hart
Robert Hart IV
Laura Fischer
Lorelei Cannon (Hachi)
Milo Spurgeon
Axel Quinn
Ayden Taylor

Cover Artist:
Lorelei Cannon (Hachi)

Somewhere in the mountains of West Virginia, a hazardous biomass was detected by Washington D.C.

Four special agents were dispatched to collect samples and return to D.C.

This is their story.

Act 1 -
The Beginning

Act 1 Characters:

Agent Matthews: 31 year old white man, wearing a suit and tie with a hidden Glock 17 tucked into his waistband. Shaggy hair.

Agent Miller: 26 year old white man, wearing a button up white shirt with a hidden Glock 17 in his waistband. Mid length well kept hair.

Agent Brown: 29 year old black man, wearing a suit and tie. Has a Glock 17 openly holstered on his hip. Buzzed hair.

Agent Davis: 30 year old white man, wearing a black suit and tie with a black button up shirt under. Has a Glock 17 tucked in his suit. Short well kept hair.

Adrian Wilkes: 24 year old white man, blonde hair, wears a stained gray T-shirt and black work pants.

Levi Baker: 34 year old white man, stubble beard with short black hair. Wears a flannel and blue jeans, carrying a 1911 pistol holstered on his hip.

Dennis: 59 year old white man, gray hair. Wearing a T-Shirt and Blue Jeans.

Jackson and Johnson: 25 year old white men, blonde hair. Jackson's is longer than Johnson's. Both are wearing solid color shirts with blue jeans.

Act 1, Chapter 1 - The Dispatch

As the propellers of the helicopter slowed to a halt, Agent Matthews, Miller, Brown, and Davis stepped off the helicopter onto the boiling pavement. As Davis took a few steps forward, he looked towards the small town that sat in front of them.

"That's where the report came from. Let's move," he said. Following his orders, the three other agents began towards the city behind him. Agent Brown reached for his radio, pushing the small button labeled "PTT".

"Washington, this is Brown with Unit 412. We've made contact with the town. Entering now."

"Copy that, 412. Report back when you make contact with the biomass. Over."

The group continued through the town. Despite it being the middle of the day, the streets were quiet. Not a soul was outside their house.

"Where is everybody?" Miller asked.

"Probably hiding from whatever this *thing* is," Matthews answered.

The four agents continued through the desolate town. Davis glanced into the sky, seeing some sort of bird-of-prey circling overhead. Looking back down, the only inhabited vehicle that they'd seen since they left the helicopter drove past them. A Ford Focus rolled down the street, a person's face pressed against the back driver's side window.

"Get out!" the muffled voice yelled, "Get out of town!!"

"What the hell..." Davis began.

"Just keep moving," Matthews said, patting him on the back as they continued towards the middle of town. When they finally arrived at a fountain, which marked the center of town, they spotted the reported Biomass.

"Washington, this is 412. We've made contact with the biomass. Moving in to take samples now."

"Copy that, report when finished."

Davis moved towards the mass. He clutched a vile in one hand, and a pocket knife in the other. He moved his hand out towards the cancerous growth in the bottom of the fountain. It seemed to have destroyed the bottom of the fountain and rooted itself into the ground beneath it.

Leaning down, he sliced at the tumor in the well. The mass squelched away from him, but he managed to get a sample into his container. The red, skin-like blob continued to wriggle as if it felt pain.

"What now?" Matthews asked.

"We get back to the recon point."

"Wait a minute," Brown said, not even turning to face the group.

"What is it?" Davis asked, approaching him. Brown lifted a finger and pointed at a man who was sitting next to, but not on, a park bench next to the fountain. Curled in a fetal position, he was clawing at his own skin like a savage animal.

"The itching, it won't go away... Help me... Help me!!" the man screamed. The group approached the man, concerned.

"What is going on, sir?" Matthews asked.

"I touched that thing in the damn fountain and now my skin... Help!" The man couldn't even finish a sentence. He fell over onto his side, continuing to claw away at himself. Flakes of dry and dead skin fell onto the gravel below him.

"What do we do?" Miller asked, turning to Davis.

“This is an effect of the biomass, we need to bring him with us,” Davis said. Davis began to reach out a hand, but before he could even make contact with the man, he lurched towards the group. Foaming at the mouth, he swung his arms wildly.

“Sir, stop!” one of the agents shouted, but he didn’t listen. He continued to attack, resulting in Matthews finally drawing his Glock 17 sidearm and firing a three round burst into the attacker.

As he fell to the ground, the group moved towards the body. They watched as the skin on his body seemed to become one with the biomass, rooting itself into the ground.

“We need to get back to Washington... now.”

Act 1, Chapter 2 - The Flee

Davis turned around, beginning to move away from the site. The other four agents began following him, until he suddenly stopped in the middle of the road.

"Oh God," Matthews began.

"You don't think they're all..?" Brown continued. In front of them stood a crowd of maybe thirty people who were all stumbling about, coughing and scratching themselves maniacally.

One of the infected caught a glimpse of the four agents standing in front of them, letting out a guttural growl. As if it alerted the other infected, they lifted their heads to look at the group.

"We need to move, now!" Miller shouted, making a break for it. Close behind him, the other three agents ran. The crowd of infected citizens continued behind them, flailing their arms crazily.

"Where are we going!?" Brown shouted, questioning the others.

"Find shelter!" Davis commanded, continuing to sprint. Eventually, Miller ran up onto a porch after turning down a side road. The other three followed him up as he pressed against it, struggling against the lock.

"How do we get inside!?" Miller beckoned.

"Keep pushing!" Davis commanded, firing several rounds from his sidearm towards the crowd of infected monsters approaching them.

"It isn't budging!" Miller screamed. The other three agents had all joined the effort to fight back. Suddenly, to everybody's surprise, the door sprang open. Miller tripped forward from his weight, pushing through the door onto the floor inside.

"Who are you!?" a voice called from inside. The rest of the agents flooded through the door and slammed it behind them.

"We're just looking for shelter–from them!" Davis explained, gesturing towards the door. The owner of the house took a step back, sighing deeply.

"What's your name?" Brown asked the resident of the house.

"Adrian. Adrian Wilkes," he responded.

"Nice to meet you, Mr. Wilkes. May we use your house for shelter?" Brown continued.

"For now, but don't think you're staying here long. And you ain't getting any of my food!" Adrian responded. He walked away from the group into a different room.

"What do we do? What do we tell *him*?" Miller asked, waving his hand towards the door Adrian had gone through.

"Well we can't tell him we're here on government business. I'll step outside and radio D.C. while you all get settled," Davis went on.

As Davis stepped outside into the fenced-in backyard, he grabbed his radio and held down on the Push To Talk button.

"This is Agent Davis with 412. The mass has infected this city's residents and turned them into mindless monsters. We have the sample, and we're taking shelter in a resident's house. Any further directions?"

There was no response. He sat holding his radio for several seconds.

"Washington, come in?" he continued.

There was still no response.

A minute passed.

No response.

Three minutes passed. There was radio static on the other end, like someone pressed the button but didn't talk.

"Washington, respond!" Davis continued, almost losing his temper.

"This is Washington. We'll send a chopper to recon with you at the drop point at dawn. Be there at first light. Washington, over and out," someone said over the radio. It was a different voice from the last times they'd radioed the capital.

Davis stepped back inside. Adrian was immediately inside the door, looking Davis up and down.

"What are you boys doin' here?" he asked in a thick country accent.

"What do you mean?" Davis asked.

"I *mean,* you clearly ain't from around here, dressed in your fancy suits with your pistols tucked," Adrian went on.

"We were just passing through, on our way to a business meeting in Charleston," Davis explained, lying.

"A business meeting? What kind of business meeting requires four men armed with Glocks?" Adrian continued probing.

"The kind where we signed a contract saying we can't talk about it," he was interrupted, Matthews walking in, "Now, what did HR say when you called them, Davis?"

"I explained the situation to them, and they said they would move the meeting to tomorrow so we can wait through the night," Davis explained. Matthews understood what he meant, turning to Adrian.

"Do you have a place we can sleep through the night?" he asked.

"I've got a guest bedroom, but it ain't gonna fit four people," Adrian answered.

"Will it fit three?" Davis asked.

"Bed'll fit two. If one of y'all wants to sleep on the couch, be my guest," Adrian went on.

"That will work. Two of us will take shifts sleeping on the couch and patrolling to make sure nobody or no*thing* gets in," Matthews said.

"Fine, it's this way," Adrian said, walking towards the guest bedroom.

Act 1, Chapter 3 - The Patrol

Davis laid, snoring gently on the couch. Miller stepped outside through the front door onto the porch. It was quiet outside, not a single infected in sight. He rested his right hand on the grip of his pistol, watching the moon float gently across the night sky.

Miller stepped down off the porch, beginning his patrol around the house. He went left, stepping through the yard as he looked for any signs of the infected, or the biomass. He rounded the corner to the backside of the house, not noticing the sounds of the inhumane gurgling sounds at first.

**

Miller stepped back inside. The sound of the door slamming woke Davis up, who immediately got to his feet.

"Your turn," Miller began. The two traded spots, with Davis going outside to patrol and Miller laying on the couch. Unlike Miller, Davis went right off the porch, He rounded to the right side of the building, continuing down the side.

He eventually reached the gate into the backyard, unlocking it and pushing it open. He stumbled across a corpse, its skin peeling and rooted into the ground–the dead body of one of the infected. One bullet hole clean between the eyes left it unmoving. As Davis finished his patrol he stepped back inside.

On the couch, he saw Miller scratching at his arms intently. Dead skin flakes covered the cushions in a powder-like film. Davis took a step back, clutching the grip of his pistol.

"Oh God, no," he began. Miller woke up, his eyes shooting around the room.

"Davis?" he seemed to beckon.

"I'm here, Miller," Davis answered.

"It touched me... that thing out there touched me... I can't stop scratching, Davis," Miller complained.

"Just stay on the couch, okay?" Davis said, his voice shaking.

He stepped outside, watching as the sun began to rise. Going back inside, he blew into the guest bedroom and shook Brown and Matthews awake.

"Huh–What's going on?" Matthews began. Brown's eyes opened groggily as he glanced up at Davis.

"Miller is infected," he whispered.

"What!? How!?" Matthews began.

"Hey, quiet! Be quiet! He was patrolling and one of those things touched him," Davis explained.

"What do we do? Is there any way to save him?" Brown began.

"Not that we know of right now! And we can't waste too much time figuring it out, or he'll turn and we'll have no choice but to defend ourselves."

"What do we tell Adrian?" Matthews beckoned.

"He deserves to know, we'll tell him when he wakes up later," Davis answered. The group returned to the living room, where Miller was lying surrounded by his own flakes of skin. The infection seemed to dry out the skin, leaving it rough, itchy, and flaky.

"Why do you think it makes their skin so dry?" Brown asked.

"Who knows? The scientists back in D.C. might be able to figure it out. And if not, they can test this sample and find a way to fix it," Davis answered.

Just then, the sound of the bedroom door opening and then closing caused all four of them to turn their heads.

Act 1, Chapter 4 - The Conflict

The four agents walked into the kitchen as Adrian walked around upstairs.

"Why do we have to tell him?" Miller asked.

"He deserves to know, we brought it into his house," Davis told him. The kitchen was out of eyesight from the stairs, so they didn't know where Adrian might have been in the house.

"Wait, what if he freaks out? Does he have any guns in the house?" Matthews began.

"The only guns I know of are the four we brought in," Davis answered. Brown interjected by clearing his throat, pointing to Miller's hip.

His gun wasn't there.

Just then, Adrian sprang around the corner and grabbed Miller by the shoulder, pulling him into a chokehold. In his hand, he held Miller's Glock. He waved it around for a second before pointing it to the side of Miller's head.

"Now, you all are going to explain what the Hell is going on! What is happening outside, and who are you four!?" Adrian shouted. Davis reached out a hand, his other above his hand in a surrendering fashion.

"Calm down, Adrian," Davis began.

"Shut up! Don't talk unless it's to tell me what's goin' on!"

"Adrian, think about what you're doing!" Matthews said.

"What do you know that I don't!?" Adrian went on.

He pushed the gun forward, pointing it at the other three now. Miller's hands shook as he raised them, his face trembling in shock and fear.

"Tell me now or I'll kill him!" Adrian shouted.

"Adrian, for the love of God... He's infected!" Davis shouted. Adrian's face went from anger to shock. Then, in a split second, to pure fear.

"What!?" Adrian yelled. In a second, he pushed Miller down to the kitchen floor. Landing face first, Miller flipped himself over to face Adrian.

"Why didn't you tell me!?" Adrian shouted.

"We were about to! We were getting ready to tell you!" Matthews yelled.

"You–You should have told me!" Adrian yelled again, his hands shaking as he pointed the gun accusingly towards the agents at the other end of the kitchen.

He took a step back, but his back slammed into the wall behind him.

"Is there a cure!?" he shouted.

"Not that we know about," Davis began.

"But even if we did, we wouldn't tell you! You just pulled a gun on us!" Matthews protested.

"This is your fault! You should have told me!" Adrian yelled, lowering the gun to point at Miller. He simply raised his hands in fear, still trembling.

Adrian panicked, scratching his arm. His panic doubled when he watched the skin fall off his arm onto the floor below.

"This is all your fault!" He shouted, pointing the gun at Miller again, this time pulling the trigger. The gunshot echoed through the kitchen, causing all three of the other agents to flinch.

"Why didn't you fucking tell me!?" he screamed, turning the gun on himself. In a split second, there were two bodies on the floor in the kitchen. Two bullet casings rolling around the tiles. Two echoing gunshots bursting through the agents' ears.

"Holy shit!" Matthews exclaimed, taking a step back. Davis stood, unwavering. He was frozen, but it was unclear if he was frozen with fear or resolve. Brown rushed forward to Miller's side.

"Get away from him!" Davis shouted, "You don't need to get infected, too!"

Brown stopped in his tracks and backed away, leaving Miller on the ground. The pool of blood around Miller's head grew, as did the one around Adrian's.

"What do we do!?" Matthews screamed. Davis raised a hand, signaling to the others to quiet down. In the silence that followed the gesture, Davis heard the gurgling and sputtering of an infected outside.

"They're out there, and they heard those gunshots," Davis began, whispering in a hushed tone.

"Oh God, they're attracted to noise!?" Matthews went on. Davis raised a hand again, trying to calm Matthews down.

"What now?" Brown asked quietly.

"We have to draw them into one place, and then escape out the other way," Davis suggested.

"No way, this house is the only safe place!" Matthews began.

"What would you rather us do?" Davis asked him.

"We have to fight!" Matthews went on.

"Fight!? We barely have enough ammo to get us out of this house, let alone fight a horde of those things!" Davis continued.

"We can't just leave the house behind!" Matthews defended.

"It's our only choice. The helicopter from D.C. will be arriving any minute now!"

"Let Brown decide," Matthews said, suggesting a tiebreaker.

"Well?" Davis asked, turning to him.

"We have to get to that chopper. I'm with Davis," Brown decided.

**

"Okay, when I say go, you drop the pots and pans in the corner of the kitchen and meet us outside," Davis said.

"Why are we sending him to do that?" Matthews asked.

"It will lure them to the other side of the building from us, so we'll have more time to escape," Davis explained. He turned to Brown and gave him the signal.

Act 1, Chapter 5 - The Escape

As the pots clattered to the ground, Davis and Matthews ran outside. Seconds later, Brown met them in the backyard and they continued away from the house. Glancing over his shoulder, Davis saw the building become surrounded by infected.

They crowded around the building like a mob, protesting against the house's very existence. Tearing at the walls, they threw the siding to the ground and pulled the screen door off its hinges.

"Glad we aren't in there now?" Davis asked Matthews as they ran away from the home.

Matthews ignored the remark, continuing towards the edge of town. The group continued through the alleyways of the town, hiding away from the groups of infected that roamed the streets.

Davis approached the side of a brick building, peering into the street around the corner. The other two began towards him, but he lifted a hand, signaling them to stop.

"What is it?" Brown began, but Davis lifted a finger to his mouth and shushed him. Davis looked out towards the street again, seeing several infected citizens coming their way.

"We need to hide," he said, turning back towards the other two agents.

"Hide? Why?" Matthews asked. Davis turned to him, pointing towards the street.

"Cause there's a crowd of those *things* coming our way!" he explained.

Davis walked back into the alley, turning down a different route. As the two followed him, they began to wonder where he was leading them. Brown looked towards Matthews, who was clearly beginning to question Davis's leadership.

"Davis, where are we going!?" Matthews beckoned.

"Wherever *they* aren't," he replied, gesturing towards the direction of the infected group. Sighing, Matthews continued following.

Eventually, the group got to another wall, which Davis peered around. Brown, who was leaning on a door, suddenly stumbled backwards, into the building under his own weight. Matthews stepped forward, looking into the building where Brown had disappeared.

"Davis, this door was unlocked!" Matthews whispered. Davis turned around and approached the door as Brown pulled himself to his feet.

"What is this?" Davis asked, walking inside.

"It's an apartment building, I think," Davis replied. They looked around for a second, seeing six doors, three on either side of the hallway. Towards the end of the hallway, a stairwell began up to the second floor.

"We should search these rooms for survivors," Matthews suggested. For once, Davis agreed with him.

"Yeah, let's start with the left side. Each one of us gets a door," Davis plotted. Matthews stood at the first door. Davis stood at the second, and Brown at the third.

"Alright, let's go!" Davis signaled, and the men breached the doors.

Act 1, Chapter 6 - The Rooms

Matthews breached into a room that was almost entirely empty. A seemingly vacant apartment stood in front of him. Matthews looked across a wide, carpeted living area. A small wooden chair sat in one of the corners, the only sign of furnishing that this apartment had ever experienced.

Despite the emptiness of the first room, he continued through the apartment into the bedroom. A bedframe with no mattress sat, slightly angled against the wall. Matthews bent at his waist to look under the frame, but it was too dark to see anything.

Deciding that there was probably nothing anyway, Matthews continued into the bathroom.

It was quite disappointing, however. The room was a barren white color, with no decorative towels or shower curtains to contrast it. The toilet seat was left down, no bathroom tissue to compliment it.

He decided to make his way back into the hallway, as his apartment was empty.

**

Davis breached into his room, which was seemingly a lived-in space. The carpeted living space in this room was complimented by a blue felt couch. In front of it, a wooden desk sat with a flatscreen television propped up on top of it.

"United States government! Anyone in this room, show yourself, now!" Davis called out. Unsurprisingly, there was no reply. However, he continued through the room anyway. He peered into a small kitchen area, which had dirty dishes in the sink. Davis's eyes darted to a door across the hall from the kitchen. He pushed it open, revealing an empty bedroom. There was a twin sized bed, the blankets spread across it disorderly.

However, the room was empty.

Davis continued to another bedroom, this one with a Queen Sized bed. It also was empty. Unlike the other, however, the bed was made and neat. As Davis had fully swept the apartment, he gave up and returned to the hallway to regroup with the others.

**

Brown breached into his apartment, which was fully decorated. A mounted taxidermy deer head overlooked the living room, accompanied by several pictures of farmhouses and barns. He got to the kitchen, which had a knife block with several professionally carved knives.

Deciding it may be useful, Brown grabbed one and tucked it into his belt. He made his way down the hallway, pushing open the door to a side room across from the kitchen. Originally intended to be a bedroom, the room had just been used for storage.

Brown continued down the hall, entering a bedroom. In the center of the room, there was a queen sized bed, complete with the messy comforter that was nearly strung onto the ground. On the other side of the bed from Brown stood a man, about six feet tall. He was wearing a plaid button-up shirt and a pair of dirty blue jeans. His face wore a scraggly black beard, a worried expression hidden behind it.

In his right hand, he held a model 1911 handgun with a blued-steel slide, pushed forward and pointed at Brown.

Act 1, Chapter 7 - The Invitation

Brown took a step back, unholstering his pistol and pointing it at the man who stood across from him.

“Woah, drop the gun!” Brown shouted, fixing his sights on the man’s torso. The other two agents, who had finished clearing their rooms by now, heard the commotion and ran into the room.

“Who are you people!?” the resident asked, his hand shaking as he pointed the gun at all three of them.

“We’re government officials, here to help with the infection that’s spreading in your town,” Davis said, reassuring the man.

“What’s your name?” Matthews asked in a calming tone.

“L-Levi,” the man stuttered, “Levi Baker.”

“Alright, Levi, would you mind putting the gun down?” Matthews went on.

“Y-You first,” Levi went on, still holding the gun out towards the agents. Accepting the offer, the agents holstered their weapons, and Levi did as well.

“Alright, now that we aren’t threatening each other anymore, would you like to come with us to Washington?” Matthews proposed.

“Wait, those aren’t our orders,” Davis objected.

“Hey, we have an open spot on the chopper since Miller won’t be joining us, and we need to save as many people from this thing as we can,” Matthews argued.

“Go to Washington? For what?” Levi asked.

"We're taking a sample of the infection to them so we can study it, hopefully find a cure," Brown explained.

"Yeah... Yeah, I'll come with you, it's not like there's much of a town left to stay in here," Levi said, accepting the invitation. Just then, a bloody handprint was spread across the window behind Levi as an infected citizen pounded against it.

"Shit, they must have heard all the yelling," Brown began.

"I've got some knives in the kitchen, sharpest you'll find this side of the Blue Ridge Mountains. It'll help us conserve ammo," Levi suggested.

"Good idea, let's grab some," Davis agreed.

The group made their way to the kitchen, Levi grabbing a knife first. He looked at the block for a second before turning to the others.

"That's weird, there's one missing," Levi said, turning around.

"I already took one on my way in," Brown acknowledged, pulling the blade from his belt.

The group made it outside, knives in hand. A couple infected stumbled up to them, prompting the group to begin slashing at them. As the group made their way out of the city, they continued cutting through groups of infected citizens.

Act 1, Chapter 8 - The Blockade

The agents made their way to the edge of the town. On the outskirts, there was a small family diner with a full parking lot. As the rest of the group began to move past it, the restaurant caught Levi's eyes.

"Man, I'm starving... can we just stop in and grab something?" Levi began.

"Uhh, I don't know if you've noticed or not, but everybody in this town is infected. The people in there will be no different," Davis objected. However, by the time he was done speaking, Levi had already entered the Diner.

"Are you kidding me?" Brown began.

Within seconds, the agents began to hear sounds of distress, the distinct sound of a glass shattering, and Levi screaming for help.

"Help! Someone get in here!" Levi wailed. Shaking his head in disbelief, Davis moved up to the door and pushed it open, his gun in one hand and his knife in the other.

The other two agents entered behind him, their weapons ready as well. Inside, Levi had jumped over the kitchen counter and was holding back an infected citizen that had climbed over it with him. Several other infected people were standing at the counter, waving their arms over it in an effort to grab at him.

Davis sprung forward, stabbing one in the back of the head. It dropped to the floor as he pulled the knife out, pushing it into another.

Brown chopped a few down, giving Levi an opening to dart through and escape. Free from the infected inside the Diner, the group ran outside. Davis turned to Levi on the way out to speak to him.

"Next time I tell you no, listen to me! Okay!?" he shouted at the new recruit.

"Okay, fine! I'm sorry!" he replied. As the two averted their eyes from each other, they slowed to a stop. Brown and Matthews also halted next to them. Just on the outside of town, right where they needed to be, at least one-hundred-and-fifty infected citizens were pacing the area.

As the group stared, an infectious tumor-like piece of the biomass rooted itself up out of the ground and sprung up around the group.

"Holy shit, they're walling us in!" Brown panicked.

"How are we gonna get past this!?" Matthews went on, turning to Davis. Spread across his face was a look of utter disbelief, almost a sense of dread. He took a step backwards and blinked rapidly.

"We'll think of something," he began.

"Well we'd better think fast!" Levi said, raising a finger to point out the blockade of infected people beginning to move inwards towards the town, towards the agents.

As the infected mass of people continued their march towards the group, the other infected citizens inside the diner began stumbling out. Some pushed through the doors, while others shattered windows and fell out onto the pavement.

"We need to think of something now!" Levi continued. He pulled the same pistol that he'd been threatening Brown with earlier, pointing it at the creatures that were beginning to limp towards him.

"Let's turn around! Go back into town!" Brown suggested.

"Are you crazy? They'll just corner us back there! The chopper's drop point is out *there*," Davis protested. A gunshot rang out as Levi blasted one of the infected, who had seemingly gotten too close to him.

"How about we-" Matthews began, but he was promptly interrupted by the sound of an engine revving. The group turned around to see a Jeep Gladiator slow to a halt in front of them.

"Y'all need a lift!?" the driver asked, leaning his head through his window.

"Yes, please!" Davis answered, running up to the side of the Jeep. Inside, the group was shocked to see two other men in the backseat.

"Is there enough room for all four of us?" Brown asked the driver.

"Eh.. pro'lly not now that I consider it. Some of you can ride in the truck bed if ya'd like," he went on.

"Matthews, Brown, you good to ride in the back?" Davis asked. The two agents nodded their heads, letting Levi climb into the backseat with the two strangers, and Davis into the passenger seat.

"Where y'all headed?" the driver asked Davis.

"The other side of that horde of infected, to the open field behind them," Davis answered.

"Gotcha," the driver said, shifting the car into drive and pulling out of the diner parking lot. He began into the street, turning right towards the horde.

"What's your name?" Davis asked the driver.

"Dennis. How 'bout yourself?" he returned.

"Agent Davis. That's our friend Levi in the back," Davis answered.

Matthews patted the glass on the back of the vehicle, which Levi slid to the side. Poking his head through, Matthews began talking.

"Hey, there are two M4 rifles in the back of this truck!" he shouted into the cab.

"Oh yeah! There should be a bag with some spare magazines in there too! Feel free to use 'em if you wanna pick off some of this horde up 'ere!" Dennis responded.

Loading a magazine into one, Matthews pulled the charging handle back and chambered a round.

"This is about to get badass," Brown said, doing the same.

"What about these two? Who are they?" Levi asked, turning to the two men in the backseat.

"I'm Jackson, that's Johnson. He don't talk much," one of them said, gesturing towards the other.

"Jackson and Johnson?" Levi asked, pointing out the similarities in their names.

"We're twins," Jackson clarified.

"You boys get ready with them rifles! Here they come!" Dennis shouted back to the two in the bed. Facing the front of the truck, the two prepared to engage their targets. Davis watched as the members of the crowd began to fall as the booms of the rifles echoed through the cab of the truck.

"Woohoo!" Dennis shouted, pulling the handbrake as he drifted the truck around the side of the blockade. Matthews stumbled as he held on, trying not to get launched off the truck.

Dropping his magazine, Brown pushed another in and chambered a new round, engaging again. Dennis slammed on the brakes, avoiding driving through the crowd of infected. Before anyone in the truck knew it, he'd shifted into reverse and was now backing up towards the town as Matthews and Brown continued dropping the enemies ahead of them.

"Alright, let's go!" Dennis said, hitting the brakes again and putting the truck back in drive. Before they'd even reached the group of infected, they all laid across the ground... dead.

"Good work, men!" Davis said as the truck pulled over in the field.

"What did you want to get into this field for?" Dennis asked as Davis climbed out of the truck.

"We've got a helicopter meeting us here to take us out of this place," Davis answered.

"Woah, can we come?" Jackson asked, stepping out of the truck, the door slamming behind him.

"There's not enough room in the chopper for that," Davis rejected.

"So we escort you around this horde, let you use up all of our ammunition, and what do we get in return, huh?" Dennis began, "A pat on the back!?"

"You offered us the ride!" Davis said, defending himself and his men.

"Where is this helicopter anyway?" Jackson asked.

"That is–actually a good question," Davis responded, grabbing his radio.

"This is Davis with 412, is that chopper inbound?"

Act 1, Chapter 9 - The Silence

There was nothing but radio static on the other side. Davis took another few steps into the field, hoping that it was just a bad signal from the area he was standing in.

"D.C. come in," he continued into the radio.

Silence.

"This is Agent Davis with unit 412. We're ready for Evac. Come in."

Silence.

"One of you try," he said, turning to Brown and Matthews.

"This is Agent Matthews, unit 412. Anybody there?"

Silence.

Silence...

Until there wasn't.

For a split second, the static was interrupted before immediately returning. Someone had pressed their push-to-talk button on their radio before quickly releasing it, as if they decided not to say whatever they planned to say.

"This is Agent Davis with the 412 Unit! Our objective is complete, and we're ready to be picked up! Come in!" Davis screamed into his radio.

Silence.

Dennis leaned to one side, his hands on his hips. A grin spread across his face.

"They ain't comin' for you, are they?" he chuckled.

"Holy shit, you're joking! You promised me a helicopter ride!" Levi said, a panicked look flooding his expression.

"What do we do now!?" Brown asked, stepping forward in front of Levi.

"Washington, respond!" Davis barked into the microphone on his radio.

"The chopper isn't coming, Davis. I'm sorry," a voice said from the other end of the radio.

"What do you mean!? Why not!?" Davis shouted again.

"Washington, over and out."

There was a click on the other end, and the silence returned.

Act 1, Chapter 10 - The Deal

Davis's hands rose to his head, holding it in disbelief.

"What do we do!?" Brown asked again.

"I'm thinking, okay!?" Davis shouted.

"Think faster, damn it!" Brown shouted back.

"Both of you shut the fuck up!" Matthews barked, stepping between them. He looked up towards Dennis, who was leaning against the door to his truck.

"Dennis, would you take us to the Capital?" Matthews asked, starting towards him.

"What's in it for me?" Dennis asked, cocking his head to the side, "You all have already made me do so much for so little."

"We'll provide you protection, help you find supplies, and get you the hell away from this town," Matthews suggested. He glared towards Brown and Davis, who were back to back, looking in opposite directions of each other.

Matthew's gaze caught Davis's attention first.

"Yes, we'll help you guys," Davis agreed.

"Yeah," Brown agreed.

Dennis looked at the ground for a second, taking a few steps away from the truck. Without looking up, he raised a finger and pointed it at Jackson and Johnson.

"What'd you think about that plan?" he asked the two.

Jackson looked at Johnson, who simply shrugged his shoulders. He looked back towards Dennis and raised a hand to his chin for only a split second before answering.

"Let's do it."

"I'll agree, but I'm adding one thing to the contract," Dennis said, stepping forward.

"What is it?" Matthews asked.

"Truck needs gas."

"We can do that, we'll figure out how," Davis responded.

"Then it's a deal," Dennis said, stepping forward with his hand ready.

Matthews grabbed it, shaking his hand and sealing the deal.

"Alright then, hop in," Dennis said, opening the door to his truck.

The group did so, Brown and Matthews getting back in the truck bed while Jackson, Johnson, and Levi got in the back. Finally, Davis climbed into the passenger seat and shut the door.

"Where'd you say that chopper was supposed to take you?"

"D.C." Davis answered.

Act 2 - The Way Back

Act 2 Characters:

Ava: 29 year old white female, wearing a purple T-Shirt and black skinny jeans. Long tangled brown hair. A look of terror covers her face.

Sergeant Wilson: 36 year old white cop. Sharp jawline, medium length black hair. Wears a grimy and tattered police uniform.

Rodriguez: 42 year old Mexican American man. Long hair, stubbly beard. Wears a tan trench coat with a pair of black work pants.

Oliver Williams: 38 year old white man. Black suit and tie, well kept black hair. Doesn't carry a firearm usually, but will if he feels threatened.

Elija Jones: 37 year old black man. Wears a pilot uniform. Usually goes by Badger Niner Niner while flying his helicopter. Not much about his appearance is known.

Act 2, Chapter 1 - Cass Road

Dennis turned the key in the ignition and the truck roared to life. The time on the dashboard read 9:27am. Seeing this, Davis began to worry that maybe they *had* sent the chopper, and the team was just late to it.

"How long is the trip to Washington?" Levi asked from the back.

"With no stops? About four and a half hours if we're lucky," Dennis answered.

"Take your time, we ain't getting there with no stops," Jackson said, leaning to where Dennis could see him through the rearview.

Dennis put the truck in drive and pulled back towards the small town that they'd just left from. He drove along some back roads for a couple of minutes before turning onto a small trail-like road.

Davis looked out the window and read a sign labeled "Seneca Trail". After a couple more minutes, the group had somehow made it onto U.S. Route 219.

"When did we get off of Seneca Trail?" Davis asked, looking at Dennis.

"Oh, uh, Seneca Trail *is* Route 219. They're the same road," Dennis explained.

"Oh, yeah I get that," Davis responded.

For around 4 minutes the truck continued weaving through the mountains. As they headed east, the sun peeked over the mountain tops. Dennis pulled his sun visor down and blocked the light from his eyes.

About a few minutes into the journey, the truck let out a harsh dinging sound that shot Levi awake in the backseat.

"What's that?" he asked, groggily. Dennis looked at the dash and rose a palm to his forehead.

"Damn it, the gas light came on. We're gonna have to pull over somewhere," Dennis answered.

"How far can we make it on E?" Jackson asked.

"Uhh, probably about 3 miles or so?" Dennis guessed.

"Are there any gas stations around?" Levi asked, wiping his eyes.

"Probably somewhere, but how far?" Davis asked. The truck continued running for about 2 minutes as they made it to a fork in the road. To their right was a street labeled "Cass Road", which Dennis turned onto. As soon as the truck made the turn, the engine cut and the truck began losing speed.

On their right, there was a parking lot with a rather large building. Dennis allowed the truck to roll into the parking lot before he hit the brakes and shifted into park.

"Why are we stopping?" Matthews asked, hopping out of the back of the truck.

"We're out of gas," Dennis said, hopping out of the truck. He put a lit cigar to his lips and took a hit before blowing the smoke through his nostrils.

"Well shit, what do we do now?" Brown asked, jumping out next to Matthews.

"Where even are we?" Levi asked, pulling himself out of the truck. He still looked pretty tired.

"We were on the road for like–ten minutes tops, how were you already asleep?" Jackson asked.

"I work late nights and *someone* interrupted my sleep this morning," he answered, looking towards Brown.

"All things considered, I think I'm the best thing that could've barged into your room this morning," Brown joked.

"The sign says we're at Elk River Snowboard and Ski," Davis said, walking back to the truck from the sign.

"Oh shit, I know where we are! There's a gas station like–two-hundred feet down the road," Levi said.

"So, are we pushing the truck down the street or bringing the gas to the truck?"

"It'd be easier to bring the gas to the truck," Dennis decided.

Act 2, Chapter 2 - Refuel

The door to the gas station swung open, Davis walking in. The door hit a small bell that dangled above the frame, ringing as he entered the building. Levi and Brown followed behind him.

Most of the lights in the building were out. There was seemingly no clerk, and no customers. The shelves looked as if they'd been ransacked–snacks scattered across them and slung onto the floor.

The door to a back room stood propped open, the door frame broken and splintered. The top hinge had snapped, leaving the bottom hinge as the only thing securing the door to the wall. Pistol drawn, Davis pulled the door out of the way and stepped into the back room.

Inside was a storage room, full of shipping crates that bottled drinks would be shipped in. Although the light was off, Davis could tell nobody was in the room. He took another step forward, noticing a splash as he stepped into some sort of liquid.

"Guys, I've got blood," Davis called out. He took a step out of the back room.

"Blood?" Levi asked.

"A puddle of it. Looks like someone was shot or stabbed, then left to bleed out on the floor," Davis theorized.

"So... no gas station attendant?" Brown asked.

"No, but the building seems to be without power, so I'm not sure how we'd pump the gas," Davis went on.

"Oh, that's simple. There should be an emergency generator somewhere back here that will get 'em going again," Levi answered, walking behind the counter. He opened a few doors while Brown and Davis listened from the store. After a few seconds, the lights flickered on and the soda machines began making sound.

"That work!?" he called out from the back.

"Yes!" Davis responded. Brown walked behind the counter and began typing on the register, authorizing for the pumps to be used.

Davis opened the store door, setting off the bell again. He gave Matthews, who was waiting outside with a gas can, a thumbs up that signaled to him that the pumps were on.

Matthews set the can on the ground, filling it with gasoline. Davis stepped outside to approach him.

"Are there any more cans?" he asked.

"Dennis and the twins went to go look through the Ski resort to see if they could find anything, I'd go ask them," Matthews answered, shutting off the gas.

"Alright, I'll take that back to the truck, you go make sure that Brown and Levi are okay," Davis said, picking up the can.

**

Setting the can by the truck, Davis made his way over to the ski lodge. He pushed through the door, which opened into a dimly lit room. He could tell that the room was rather large. Suddenly, he saw two beams of light cut through the darkness.

"Found 'em!" Dennis called out. A third beam of light came from a different direction. Davis watched as the other two followed Dennis's voice–and his light–to wherever the gas cans were.

Stepping back outside, Davis began pouring the gas into the truck's tank. Dennis, Johnson, and Jackson all came out of the building with two gas cans each. Making their way back to the gas station, they sat them down to let Matthews continue filling.

“We’ve got seven gas cans, each holds two gallons of gas,” Dennis began, “the truck holds twenty-two.”

“I already put one in it,” Davis said.

“Alright, that’s three trips,” Brown said. Matthews began filling every single can, one at a time.

When all seven were filled, the group took them back to the truck to pour into the tank. Then, when they were empty, they were brought back to Matthews.

It was 3:00 pm when the cans were filled for the second time. Again, the group brought them all back and filled the tank. Now, fifteen gallons had been put in the tank, seven more left.

By 4:00, the tanks were filled for a third time. The other six carried the cans back while Matthews put the nozzle back on the pump. After they were all poured in, Dennis hopped in the driver seat and put the key in the ignition.

“Woohoo! From E to F, baby!” he hollered as the engine roared.

“Back on the road, then?” Davis asked as he climbed into the passenger seat.

Act 2, Chapter 3 - Cass Mass

The group had only been on the road again for about 20 minutes. Brown and Matthews laid in the truck bed, gazing up at the sky. Levi looked out the window and saw a sign reading "Welcome to Cass".

"Hey, I think we're coming up on a city," he said to the others.

"Yeah, Cass. It's the city this road's named after. I've ain't heard much about it, actually," Dennis said.

"Isn't there a state park there?" Davis asked, turning to Dennis.

"Not quite the state park you're thinking of," Dennis answered.

Moments later, the vehicle pulled into the town. Similar to the small town that the agents had been dropped in, the city was run down. Windows were shattered, streets were quiet, and infected citizens roamed the city.

When they got to the state park, there was a sign that read "Cass Scenic Railroad State Park" with an arrow pointing towards it. A large run down train sat on the tracks, with a beautiful forest behind it.

"Want to stop and look at it?" Dennis asked the group.

"Why not," Levi said, accepting the invitation.

"Sure," Davis said.

"Yeah, let's do it," Jackson answered.

The truck pulled over, everybody getting out. They walked down into the park for a moment when Davis suddenly stopped.

"What is it?" Levi asked, turning around to face him.

"Holy shit," Davis said, raising a finger towards the large body of water. In the middle of it, another disgusting biomass poked out of the water. Among it were several fleshy tentacles, waving through the air. A bird flew above it, and one of the tentacles grabbed it out of the air.

Within seconds, the bird was pulled down into the water and submerged, never to be seen again.

"What do we do about it?" Matthews asked, staring at the mass.

"There's nothing we *can* do about it... but it means that it's spreading," Davis answered.

"They were rooting themselves into the ground, they must be burrowing under the country," Brown examined.

Suddenly, a plethora of infected citizens began pulling themselves out of the water. As quickly as they'd shown up, they fixed their eyes on the group and began towards them.

"Uh oh, that isn't good," Dennis observed.

"Back in the truck!" Jackson shouted. The group scrambled back to the vehicle, Matthews and Brown grabbing their rifles to begin picking off members of the horde.

The truck started and pulled forward about five hundred feet before Dennis slammed on the brakes. A minivan had pulled out in front of the truck, several armed men jumping out.

"Woah, what the hell!?" Dennis asked. Brown and Matthews turned around to see the group who'd stopped them.

"Hey, drop the fuckin' guns!" one of the men yelled.

"Alright, alright! Just don't shoot!" Matthews said, lowering his rifle into the bed of the truck.

"All of y'all! Get out of the truck!" the man shouted, his gun still pointed at Dennis. Compliantly, the doors of the truck swung open.

"Levi, do you still have that pistol?" Davis asked quietly as they stepped down.

"Yeah, it's on my right hip," he answered.

"Okay, follow my lead," Davis plotted.

"Where you boys headed?" the man in charge asked, stepping up with his gun at his side. All of the men were standing next to the vehicle, their hands above their heads.

"Virginia," Dennis lied. The bandit's eyes moved across the group, examining them. Davis stood slightly in front of Levi's right side, blocking the weapon from sight.

"Ask 'em if they've got any more guns!" another man from the group of bandits asked.

"You heard him," the man in front said.

"No, the rifles are the only ones," Davis began.

"That so?"

"Yes, of course."

"What about that one!?" he said, pointing an accusing finger at Brown. In his waistband, the grip of his Glock 17 was sticking out, revealing the truth.

"Levi, now!" Davis said, jumping out of the way. Quickly drawing the pistol, Levi fired a volley of shots at the leading bandit. One struck him in the throat, causing him to drop to his knees.

"Cover!" Jackson shouted, diving behind the truck. Brown and Matthews climbed back into the bed, grabbing their rifles and opening fire on the remaining bandits.

Johnson, Davis, and Dennis all followed Jackson's lead, hiding behind the vehicle. There were only a couple gunshots from the minivan's direction before the shooting stopped.

A second later, the shooting began again. However, the familiar sound of the bullets pinging off of the truck's cold metal was no longer present.

"What are they shooting at?" Dennis asked, beginning to peak out of cover.

"Oh fuck, look!" Jackson yelled, pointing at the horde of creatures marching towards the truck.

"Matthews, Brown, shoot at the infected!" Davis commanded.

"On it!" Brown shouted, turning his muzzle towards the crowd. A minute passed of continuous fire, only brief rests as a weapon was reloaded. Within two or three minutes, all of the infected were laying on the ground, motionless.

As soon as one threat was dealt with, the other returned. The crisp sound of a bullet slamming into the truck's windshield rang through Brown and Matthews's ears. The glass fracturing sent the bullet spinning, causing it to protrude through the back window. As it exited the vehicle, it missed Matthews by less than a foot.

"Shit, heads up!" Brown shouted, turning and firing back at the bandits. There were fifteen more seconds of fire before Brown raised a hand, signaling to stop.

"I think they're all down," he called.

With their guns drawn, Davis and Levi approached the vehicle. The leader, who Levi had shot in the throat, still laid on the ground. Now, he had been torn apart by infected.

"Jesus Christ," Levi said, looking at the remains.

"You, in the van!" someone called out. Davis turned and saw Dennis approaching the driver's side door of the van.

"Got a live one!" Dennis said, pulling the woman out of the van. The terrified driver raised her hands, shaking in fear.

"What was all this!?" Dennis barked at her.

"They came three days ago... They robbed me, forced me to rob others. They told me to pull out in front of you, they had me at gunpoint! I had no choice!" the woman screamed.

"Hey, calm down, it's okay," Davis reassured her. He put a hand on her shoulder and began to pull her away from the van.

"You guys, get all of *them* out of here," he said, turning around and gesturing towards the bodies that littered the area.

Act 2, Chapter 4 - On the Road Again

As the lady calmed down, the agents and the other men carried the bandits' bodies away, dumping them in the lake where the biomass was growing. Eventually, Davis came back with the lady to introduce her to the group.

"This is Ava, we're taking her with us," Davis began.

"Can we take her van?" Dennis asked.

"Yeah, I'll be driving up with you," Ava clarified.

"Looks like you two don't have to ride in the bed anymore," Dennis said, turning to Brown and Matthews.

"Awesome," Matthews said, climbing into the back seat of the van.

Brown followed, with Davis getting back in the passenger seat of Dennis's Jeep.

"I know the route, I'll lead you," Dennis called to Ava as she started her van. Dennis did the same in the truck, buckling his seatbelt as he shifted the truck into drive.

Following closely behind, Ava turned back onto the road. Dennis turned back on to Cass Road and began the drive as Ava followed with Brown and Matthews.

"So what's y'all's story anyway?" Dennis asked Davis as they continued down the road.

"What do you mean?" Davis replied, turning to him.

"Well, you introduced yourself as Agent Davis... and three men dressed in formal attire ain't exactly Blue-Ridge-Mountain typical," Dennis explained.

"We were dispatched in that town to collect a sample of the biomass, for research. A man named Oliver Williams sent us," Davis explained.

"So, you're government agents?" Dennis inquired.

"Yeah, and Williams was just going to leave us in that town without a way home," Davis continued.

"So I'm taking you back so y'all can find out why?"

"Exactly."

"Hey, Davis?" a voice over his radio beckoned. It was Brown's voice from the vehicle behind them.

"Go ahead," Davis spoke into the mic.

"Ava says that someone is coming up behind us pretty fast," Brown said.

Davis looked in the side view mirror, leaning over to see past the side of the truck. Sure enough, a rusty Chevy truck was speeding up the side of the road next to them, and was catching up.

"What do you think they want?" Dennis asked, turning to Davis slightly.

"I'm not sure, but don't stop driving," Davis said. With one hand, he began rolling down the window. With his other, he fished his pistol out of his waistband.

The truck finally caught up with them, the driver rolling down his window as well. Matching speeds with Dennis, the driver called out.

"Where ya headed!?" the man bellowed. Davis shifted in his seat, placing the pistol in his lap.

"What's it matter to you?" Davis returned.

"Cause you're heading into *my* hills," the driver responded.

"*Your* hills?"

"Damn straight. And I'll be damned if I'm gonna let some truck full of fancy-pants city boys roll into my hills," he retorted.

"We're just passing through, sir," Davis assured him.

"Bullshit," the driver replied, a smirk on his face. Just then, the back window rolled down and a man popped up. In his hand, he clutched a bolt action rifle, pointed aggressively towards the truck.

"Pull over, fancy-Dan," the driver said, chuckling.

"Sorry, man, but we've got places to be," Davis responded.

"Ava, get the hell out from behind us," he said into his radio quietly.

"You'd better pull over," the man with the rifle warned.

Ava did as she'd been told, pulling up alongside the other side of the truck. Davis looked over at her before returning his attention to the hostile truck.

"Actually... why don't you pull over?" Davis asked rhetorically. As if this scenario had been discussed prior, Dennis slammed on the brakes. The other truck sped away for a second before also hitting their brakes. A shot was fired from the rifle, but the sudden stop had thrown off the raider's aim.

Just then, a second shot was fired from Davis's sidearm. Then a third. Just like that, the enemy truck no longer had any occupants.

Wiping a drop of sweat from his forehead, Dennis hit the gas again and proceeded down the road.

"The hell did they want?" Matthews asked over the radio.

"Who knows? Probably to rob us," Davis responded.

"Where's our next stop?" Levi asked, rubbing his eyes. He'd been shaken awake by the sudden brake-slam and the gunshots, and let out a large yawn.

"Well shit, apparently right here," Dennis said. Davis looked up to see a sign that said "City of Petersburg, West Virginia" across it. About a hundred or so yards past it, a pileup of cars sat. From one end of the road to the other, cars had been parked bumper to bumper, restricting anybody from entering–or exiting–the city.

"What the fuck?" Jackson exclaimed, scooting forward in his seat.

As the truck slowed to a stop in front of the blockade, a man jumped over one of the cars. He had a rifle, but it sat neatly slung on his back.

With one hand out, he approached the truck and signaled Dennis to roll his window down. Compliantly, Dennis lowered the window and turned to look at the man as he approached him.

"Hello, my name is Sergeant Wilson with the Petersburg Police Department. Unfortunately because of an illness going around inside city limits, we aren't allowing anybody in or out," he said.

"Illness? Look, man, that 'illness' is infecting the entire country. Your little quarantine isn't stopping anything," Dennis informed him.

"I'm just doing what the chief told me," Wilson responded.

"How long has it been since the chief gave you these orders?" Dennis asked.

"Six hours," Wilson responded.

"And have you talked to him since then?"

"No, sir."

Davis leaned over and looked out the window, an ID card clutched in his hand.

"Sir, I'm a government agent. I'm asking kindly that you let us pass," he said, handing the license to the officer. Wilson examined it for a moment before handing it back over to Davis.

"Well, I'm sorry Mister Davis, but I can't let you through here," he said.

There was a moment of silence between both parties before they were interrupted. A shot rang out, and a bullet landed on the pavement next to Wilson.

"Holy shit!" Dennis shouted, ducking down in his seat.

Everyone took cover, including the members in Ava's van. A group of men ran out of the woods as Wilson made a break for it. Despite the downpour of bullets headed his way, he seemed to have made it out.

"Who are you all?" Dennis asked as one of them approached the window of the truck.

"I could ask you the same question," the man approaching the window said through clenched teeth.

"We're just passing through," Davis said, trying to calm the nerves.

"What was all that? Why'd you shoot at that officer?" Dennis asked, prying at the armed gunmen.

"The city police have been holding us and our people hostage within city limits. We're a rebellion, trying to free our people," the rebel answered, glancing back and forth from Dennis to Davis.

"Sounds like you could use our help, and we need to get through," Davis responded, negotiating with the man.

The rebel stared at the ground for a moment before waving his arms, signaling them to follow.

"This way, we'll take you around this blockade," he said. Him and his men walked off the side of the road, the truck slowly rolling behind them. Behind the truck, Ava's van also followed.

Act 2, Chapter 5 - Petersburg, West Virginia

Inside the city limits, the rebels met up with another group, who was patrolling in a wide-body Ford truck. One of the men in the back of the truck pointed out the Gladiator and the minivan tailing them.

"Who're they?" the man asked, gesturing.

"Some passer-throughers who think they can help us with the police," the rebel in front explained to his friends.

"Let's bring 'em to base then."

Now following the Ford, the group made their way through the streets of Petersburg. While some citizens were alive around the streets, many of them were infected. An infected citizen limped out from an alleyway, towards the convoy.

"Weapons hot," one of the rebels said. A second later, three pops echoed through the alley and the infected citizen fell to the ground.

"We're clear," the gunner said, signaling to the others to proceed.

"Alright, let's move," Dennis said, pulling into the alley as the other vehicle did. About fifty feet down the alleyway, the Ford slowed to a stop.

The doors swung open, the rebels stepping out from the vehicle. One of them approached Dennis's truck, his weapon in his hand.

"What's going on?" Dennis asked as the window rolled down.

"This building is our headquarters, there's someone in there you need to talk to," the rebel explained.

All the doors on the Jeep and the minivan swung open, the members of 412 stepping out and onto the pavement. They made their way to the door, following the rebels in front of them.

"Right this way," one said. He swung the door open and revealed a dimly lit warehouse. Proceeding through the building, the agents made notice of the military-grade vehicles that were parked throughout it.

"What do we do with 'em," one rebel asked the other.

"We're gonna show 'em to Rodriguez, see what he wants to do with 'em," the other answered.

The group eventually reached a staircase, a door at the top of it. The rebels led the way up, the group behind them. Dennis turned to Ava, who looked somewhat frightened.

"What's wrong?" he asked her.

"This has to be a set up... Last time I was taken to some rebel leader, he kidnapped me and forced me to drive his little bandit gang around in my van," she said, her voice quivering.

"I'm sure it'll be fine, Davis'll make sure we're on each other's side," Dennis reassured her.

The leading rebel knocked on the door twice before a voice from inside called out.

"Come in!"

The rebel pushed the door open and stepped inside, the other rebel following him.

"What is it?" the voice inside asked.

"We found some people, a group trying to pass through the city. They said that they'd help us with the police if we help them get through," a rebel explained.

"Let them in," the voice inside said. The rebels turned around and held the door open. One by one, the team made their way inside the office. A desk sat with a map sprawled out across it.

Behind the desk sat a Mexican-American man wearing a trench coat and black jeans.

"So you want to help with my rebellion, *amigos*?" the man behind the desk asked.

"Yes sir, we're willing to help," Davis answered.

"Well, if you're willing to help, I'm willing to help. I don't force anybody into my rebellion. Everybody here is a volunteer," Rodriguez went on.

"What exactly is it that you need help with?" Matthews asked.

**

A garage door rolled open. The rebels stood among Unit 412, looking out across the city. Out there, buildings stood in ruins. Police sirens flooded the streets and gunshots rang through the city.

"The cops are keeping us in the city against our will. They're infringing on our rights over an infection that we've been told has spread across the country," Rodriguez explained.

"And you want to take them down so they'll let you out," Brown stated.

"Bingo," Rodriguez exclaimed, turning to him.

"Where do we start?" Levi asked.

"We're marching on the police station tomorrow," a rebel informed him.

"Then let's get some sleep," Davis said.

The rebels showed Unit 412 to their cots, where they laid down and began to rest.

"First thing tomorrow morning, boys. You're part of a militia now. We're up at dawn!"

**

"Rise and shine, men! We're marching on the station!" Rodriguez shouted into the bunk. The agents, used to this kind of treatment, immediately got to their feet.

Dennis, Levi, and Ava all jumped in fear. Jackson and Johnson stirred a bit before pulling themselves out of their beds. Within an hour, all the men were ready and geared. The vehicles rolled out, moving towards the police station.

Dennis drove the truck with Matthews and Brown in the back again. In their hands, they clutched their M4 rifles that they'd restocked the ammo for. Ava had added sheet metal armor to her truck that Levi had helped her with. In her van, Davis and Levi had rifles that the rebels had given them.

Jackson and Johnson rode with Rodriguez, who was in a military Humvee. At the end of the road they drove on, a large police station sat. Jackson looked out a window on the vehicle, seeing an infected citizen ripping a man apart and eating his remains.

"Holy shit, this is getting crazy! They're eating people now?" Jackson exclaimed.

"Ha! People have been eating each other in these streets since the city was founded," a rebel in the front seat laughed.

"Alright, we're getting close! Prepare for contact!" Rodriguez called. His voice echoed through the radios on every man's shoulder, including the agents.

"Here we go!" a rebel shouted.

"Keep an eye out for–" someone said over the radio. Their voice cut out halfway through the sentence as a gunshot rang out through the block.

"Snipers!" someone else shouted into the microphone, finishing the now deceased man's sentence.

The vehicles swerved to the sides of the road, dodging as more rounds flew through the streets. A small army of police officers swarmed out of the front of the station.

"Out of your vehicles!" Rodriguez ordered over the radio. The door to Dennis's truck swung open as he jumped out from it. He ran around the truck and hid behind it as Matthews and Brown fired at the swarm of hostiles.

Ava, Davis, and Levi all poured out of the van, using the side as cover. Rodriguez, who'd swerved to the same side of the road as Ava, waved them over to his truck.

"Hey, we're gonna move on that sniper team, you guys are with us!" he called out to them. The three of them made their way over to Rodriguez, who pointed towards a building.

"The shot came from that rooftop, I saw the glare from the scope a second before he shot," he said. The three of them darted in between the building they sat in front of and the one next to it.

Searching the alley for a door, Ava noticed a fire escape with a ladder that had been dropped into the street.

"We can take that up!" she said, pointing to it. Following her lead, the rebels, Davis, and Levi climbed up behind her.

Meanwhile, Matthews took a couple shots at the crowd of cops that were in the street in front of the group.

"We're too far! Dennis, you're gonna have to drive us closer!" Brown called out.

"Are you crazy!? They'll gun me down before I'm a block away!" Dennis called back.

"It's the only choice! Just duck down and hold the wheel straight!" Brown told him.

"If I die here, you're gonna be the first one I eat when I come back!" Dennis shouted, climbing back into the truck. Leaning across the armrest and holding the wheel straight, Dennis shifted into drive and floored it towards the station. From the back of the truck, Matthews and Brown opened up on the crowd.

As Ava reached the top of the ladder, she climbed onto the roof and crouched down. She lifted a finger and pointed towards a man who stood on the rooftop. His back was turned to them, so it gave the squad of rebels a perfect opportunity.

"Look out!" Rodriguez called, signaling for his men to get down. A second sniper fired across the gap between the roofs, the round slamming into the roof that the rebels stood on.

Now, both snipers were aware of the rebel attackers on the roof, and were holding their sights on the cover that they hid behind.

The truck was taking heavy fire, the police blasting it as it barrelled towards them.

Similar to how he'd done in the small town that he'd found the agents in, he began driving in circles around the crowd of officers. Brown and Matthews, taking advantage of themselves being moving targets, blasted all of the officers down.

On the rooftop, Rodriguez threw a brick that he found out from behind the cover. He heard two cracks before the brick split in half.

"Both of them fired, move now!" Rodriguez yelled. He and his men ran out from behind the cover as the snipers panicked, struggling to operate their bolts.

Davis put a round in the first sniper's chest using his pistol, which caused him to fall to the ground. One of the rebels ran up and grabbed the rifle, wrestling it away from him. The other sniper across the gap managed to fire another shot, but it hit the sniper that was being wrestled rather than the rebel.

Finally, he pried the rifle out of the sniper's arms and pointed it at the other sniper, firing a round clean between his eyes. Rodriguez looked down from the rooftop, seeing Dennis and his truck circling the crowd.

"Wow, they're tearing those *pendejos* to hell!" Rodriguez exclaimed.

"*Pendejos*?" Levi asked, turning to him confused.

"Oh uh... How do you say?" he asked, turning to one of his rebels, "Oh, assholes!"

"Ah, got it," Levi said. By the time that the team had made it back to the ground, the crowd of officers had been cleared out.

"Alright, move in!" Rodriguez shouted. All of the rebels moved from their cover to the doors of the police station.

"Breach! Breach!" he ordered. The rebel in front kicked the door in, the agents following closely behind him.

Bullets began flying, several rebels going down. Brown and Matthews cleared the room, leaving one lone officer in the corner with his hands up.

"Sergeant Wilson! We should've killed you on the highway!" one rebel barked. The same officer who'd stopped 412 from proceeding through the city stood with his hands above his head.

"Where's the Chief!?" Rodriguez asked Wilson.

"Through the door!" Wilson asked, his voice shaking like a leaf in the wind.

Rodriguez kicked the door in, firing at the man on the other side with a revolver that he clutched in his hand.

"What do we do with him?" A rebel asked Rodriguez, gesturing towards Wilson.

"Please don't kill me! I'll help you! I was only doing what I was ordered to do!" he beckoned, pleading for his life.

"We'll bring him with us, then we'll decide," Rodriguez said. He grabbed a pair of handcuffs from a nearby officer and locked them around Wilson's wrists.

**

"I'm telling you, I think Rodriguez would be a good asset to the squad," Brown told the other members of Unit 412, now back at the rebel HQ.

"He fought well, and he was fighting to get out of here. We could use him," Davis agreed.

Davis made his way over to Rodriguez, who was leaning against the wall. Most of the rebels were standing around, discussing what they were going to do now that they were free to leave Petersburg.

"Hey, Rodriguez," Davis began, approaching him.

"Yes, what is it?" Rodriguez asked, turning to the agent.

"Would you and some of your rebels like to help us get to Washington D.C. to confront the government? We're also dealing with a city under siege and we were abandoned by our people," Davis proposed.

"Hmm. Let me ask my people," Rodriguez decided.

Davis walked back to his group as Rodriguez made his way to the other rebels.

"What will we do with Wilson if we go with them?" one rebel asked.

"Bring him, he might be useful," another suggested.

Rodriguez agreed with the idea, and began to make his way to the others.

"We'll come with you, but we're bringing Sergeant Wilson. Some of my men think he may come in handy," Rodriguez informed them.

"Alright, let's get going then," Dennis said, grabbing the keys to his truck. All of the rebels got to their vehicles, forming a convoy that Dennis led. Davis got in Ava's van with Levi while Brown, Matthews, Jackson, and Johnson rode with Dennis.

The journey began again, the convoy heading Eastbound on 220.

Act 2, Chapter 6 - Moorefield, West Virginia

Within an hour, the convoy had made it inside the city limits of Moorefield. This time, the group was lucky to not run into a police blockade, but what they found was equally as dreadful.

Another biomass was growing from the middle of town. All of the citizens had been infected, and tentacles similar to the ones in the Cass lake rose from the ground. As they rose, they punched through the concrete into the air.

"This is a disaster," Rodriguez began.

"No shit, this is worse than Petersburg," Wilson agreed.

Suddenly, a helicopter flew overhead, kicking up the ash and dust that had settled on the ground. It continued flying for a moment before turning around to hover over the vehicle convoy.

"What the hell is this?" Dennis asked.

"Stop your vehicles!" a voice called out from the chopper.

"Don't listen to 'em, keep going!" Rodriguez ordered over the radio.

"Convoy, stop your vehicles now or face termination!" the voice called out again. Obediently, Rodriguez stopped his vehicle, and the following vehicles followed his lead.

The helicopter lowered itself in front of the convoy, in front of Dennis's truck. A side door opened, and a man in a suit jumped out.

"Who the hell is that?" Ava asked.

"Williams," Davis began, glaring at the man.

Williams stood outside with a megaphone, his eyes looking through the windshield of every vehicle in the convoy.

"This convoy is being shut down!" Williams shouted in the megaphone.

"Shut down? What?" Dennis began, despite the fact that Williams couldn't hear him.

"Get the hell out of our way, Williams," Davis shouted, his door now open with him leaning out of it.

"Holy shit, Davis is that you? I should have known you'd make it out of that town," Williams went on, now focused on the man hanging out of the van.

"You're gonna get out of our way and tell us why you left us there!" Davis shouted.

"We picked up the signal of a large convoy headed East the second you left Petersburg. Whatever you're doing, it's over. All of you need to separate, now!" Williams shouted.

"You don't have any authority over us anymore, Williams!" Brown shouted at him through a rolled down window.

"Maybe not, but these men follow my orders. Deal with them," Williams said, climbing back into the chopper. As it took off, four men jumped out dressed similar to the agents of 412.

"Who the hell are these guys?" Matthews asked.

"Our replacements, I'd suppose," Brown responded. Dennis looked back at the men in his truck.

"You two have killed more men than this in seconds, give 'em hell!"

He slammed his foot to the gas, squealing his tires as he took off. The men drew their pistols, firing at the truck. Brown and Matthews, leaning out their windows, fired at the group of men.

Two of them went down immediately, bullets hitting their chests. The other two began falling back to cover, firing at the truck still.

"Let's go, forget them!" Davis yelled over the radio. The rest of the convoy followed Dennis, stepping on the gas and escaping from the Unit.

"That asshole–he betrayed us, left us for dead, and replaced us!" Davis shouted, punching the dashboard.

"You don't need him anymore, you've got all these people following *your* command now," Ava assured him.

"You're right... and I'm taking the fight to that bastard," Davis said, wiping his forehead.

Act 2, Chapter 7 - Major Roadblock

The group continued, following the route that Dennis had in his mind. They were on the road for about another hour when they began passing through a small city.

"What is this place?" Levi asked Davis.

"Hell if I know, I didn't see any signs," Davis replied.

The road twisted and turned through the town, but Dennis seemed to know where he was going. That was, until he slammed on his brakes. Ava had to do the same, nearly rear-ending the truck.

"Look at the size of that thing!" he shouted. In front of them stood another biomass that had burrowed out of the Earth. The only differences between this one and the last one they'd seen was the size. It was nearly twice, maybe three times as large.

"How the hell do we get around it?" Davis asked over the radio.

"Can we all go off road?" Rodriguez asked.

"I don't think Ava's van can handle that," Levi responded.

While they were coming up with a plan, the familiar sound of helicopter propellers became audible as a chopper flew over them.

"Oh great, this dickhead is back," Dennis began.

"You all look like you could use some help!" a voice that nobody had heard before called over the radio.

"Who is this? How did you get this frequency?" Davis demanded.

"Calm down, man! You want help with the cyst or not?" the voice went on, beckoning for an answer.

"Whatever you can do to help, we'd be thankful for," Matthews informed him.

"Alright, watch this!" the pilot began. Several rockets fired out from his chopper, blasting into the side of the mass. The explosions rang out, shaking the vehicles on the ground with every blast.

After several direct hits, the mass began spewing an awful bloody liquid. As it continued, the mass seemed to shrink as if it was being drained. Despite this, the helicopter continued firing until it was fully gone. Left where it was, a large biological platform branched the gap in the concrete.

"Thanks for the help," Davis said over the radio.

"No problem! Where are you all headed anyway?" the pilot asked.

"D.C." someone informed him.

"Ooh, they won't like that! Capital has been shut down for days now, ever since this started happening," the pilot informed them.

"What do you mean?" Brown asked over the radio.

"I mean every way in or out has been shut off. D.C. is the only place in the country that isn't infected yet," the pilot continued.

"We need to get into the city," Davis said.

"Well, you'll need my help," the pilot said.

"Yes, we will. What's your name, pilot?" Rodriguez asked.

"Elija Jones, but you can call me Badger Niner Niner," the pilot said, introducing himself. The convoy continued over the remains of the mass, proceeding down the road with Badger Niner Niner now watching over them.

"So what's your story, Niner Niner?" Matthews asked.

"I was a pilot for the airforce, that was before some mad man started ordering us to execute mass crowds of civilians in containment areas," he began.

"Williams, I'm assuming?" Ava asked, turning to Davis.

"Most likely," Davis agreed.

"Anyway, I abandoned the airforce and decided to start helping survivors in the remains of the country," Niner Niner finished.

"There aren't enough people in the world helping others anymore," Matthews began over the radio.

"Precisely," Niner Niner agreed. Back on the road, Unit 412 departed from the city with their new member to back them up.

Act 2, Chapter 8 - Harrisonburg, Virginia

"We're low on gas again," Dennis began, looking at his gas gauge.

"How the hell did that happen? We just filled it up!" Davis responded through the radio. One of the rebels spotted something, pointing it out to Rodriguez.

"There's a hole in your gas tank, Dennis!" the rebel leader called over the radio.

"Shit, what!?" Dennis shouted. He pulled to the side of the road, killing the engine. As he stepped out of the truck, he checked out the area behind his back tire. Just as he'd been told, a steady stream of gasoline was pouring out of a bullet-sized hole onto the ground around them.

"How the hell are we going to patch this?" Jackson asked, also looking at the leak.

"Epoxy glue, we're gonna need epoxy glue," Dennis said.

"We're in the middle of nowhere, how are we going to get epoxy glue?" Levi asked, having gotten out of Ava's van and walked over.

"What's going on down there?" Badger Niner Niner's voice asked over the radio.

"One of our ground units has a hole in his gas tank, gonna need epoxy glue to fix it. You got any?" Rodriguez asked over the radio.

"No, but I know where to get some," Niner Niner responded.

"Where at?" Davis asked.

"There's a town called Harrisonburg in Virginia about an hour south of here–an hour if you drive. I could probably be there and back in less than an hour," Badger answered.

"Land the chopper and take one of us with you," Rodriguez told him. As he was told, Badger Niner Niner put the bird down just in front of the truck that had stalled. Davis climbed aboard, waving back to his men.

"We'll be back in an hour or so!" he called to them.

**

Within thirty minutes, Davis was looking out over Harrisonburg. A home improvement store stood in ruins, infected citizens crowding around it. Davis knew that there'd be no way to go in through the front door.

"You're gonna have to drop me on the roof!" Davis called to his pilot.

"Got it!" Niner Niner responded, hovering over the building. He began lowering the altitude as Davis prepared to jump.

"Stay close," Davis ordered him as he jumped, a rope in his hand. He landed on the roof as the helicopter pulled away, hanging back in the air. Davis threw a brick through a skylight, destroying the glass and leaving him an opening to climb through.

He then tied one end of the rope to a sturdy looking post on the top of the building. After giving it a firm tug to ensure it was strong enough, he threw the other end through the broken skylight.

"This is Davis, I'm entering the building," he said over the radio.

"Copy that, Davis. Things look good out here," Badger informed him.

Davis lowered himself into the building, heading for the aisle labeled "Epoxy Adhesives". Several infected citizens roamed the halls of the store, and Davis couldn't manage to stay out of all of their sightlines.

He quickly swiped a tube of glue off of the shelf, ducking under the arms of an infected man. As he sprinted back to the rope, he grabbed his radio.

"This is Agent Davis, I'm compromised. Prepare for an immediate evacuation!"

He grabbed the rope, beginning to pull himself up. However, the infected behind him did the same. With only a foot or two between him and the infected below him, he had no time to stop and catch his breath. He had to continue pulling himself up. When he finally reached the roof, he grabbed the rope and sliced through it with the knife that he'd taken from Levi's home, dropping the rope and the infected back into the store.

Waiting for him on the roof, the helicopter had landed. Davis ran to it, jumping in as quickly as he could.

"Did you get the glue?" Elija asked.

"Yeah, I got the glue."

It was still within the hour that Davis had promised when the helicopter touched down in front of the convoy. Davis got out and headed over to the truck, where Dennis was sitting on the hood.

"You got it?" he asked as Davis approached him.

"Yeah, here it is," Davis said, handing the glue to him.

"We were... pretty lucky!" Dennis said as he bent down to apply the glue.

"Why's that?" Davis asked him.

"Well, the bullet hit pretty high up, so it didn't drain as much of our gas as I thought. We were also lucky the bullet didn't hit anything made of metal," Dennis said as he smoothed out the glue.

"You good now?"

"Yeah, that should hold! Thanks, Davis," Dennis said, shaking the agent's hand.

"No problem, let's get moving," Davis responded.

Act 2, Chapter 9 - Gainesville, Virginia

Around two hours later, the convoy had crossed the border from West Virginia into Virginia. A large town on Interstate 66 called Gainesville stood in front of them. I-66 ran straight through the middle of the city, and was the road that the convoy continued along.

That was, until, a blockade similar to the police barrier that the convoy had met in Petersburg blocked their way.

"Great, another band of assholes blocking the damn highway," Rodriguez said, an angry tone in his voice.

"You think they're cops?" Matthews asked over the radio.

"No," Wilson began, "We're already halfway through the city. These people aren't trying to keep anybody out of the city, just trying to stop people on the highway."

Dennis's truck slowed to a stop in front of the pileup of cars. Rather than a police officer jumping out at them this time, a band of civilians jumped out with guns drawn.

"Put the fucking guns down!" Brown shouted as he and Matthews leaned out the windows with their rifles.

"Hey, get back in the damn truck!" one of the raiders shouted.

"I'd listen to them, assholes!" Dennis shouted at the bandits. A couple of rebels got out of their vehicles and approached the band of men.

"Hey, I'm gonna start shooting fuckers!" the pirate called out.

"Do that shit and you're all dead," Brown ordered.

"Davis, do you want me to obliterate these assholes?" Badger Niner Niner asked from above.

"No, don't engage, we're too close to them," Davis ordered.

There was a multi-way standoff now. Some of the raiders had guns pointed at Dennis, Brown, and Matthews. Some of them were aimed at the rebels. The rebels were aimed at the raiders. Multiple drivers of several vehicles had their weapons drawn as well.

"You assholes are gonna get out of our way. Now!" Brown ordered them.

"Fuck! You!" the raiders yelled back.

"Have it your way, asshats," Matthews began. The second his finger touched the trigger, though, shots began flying. Two or three rebels went down in seconds. Matthews and Brown had to duck back into the truck as they avoided being shot.

"Shit, move!" Davis yelled. He opened the door to Ava's van and jumped out as a bullet pinged off the metal sheeting.

Levi jumped out the other way, sending a .45 round clean through a bandit's chest. As the rounds continued flying, more bandits showed up from behind the blockade.

One bandit ran at Davis, who squeezed off a couple rounds at him. However, the bandit's unpredictable zig-zagging prevented the rounds from hitting their target. Davis squeezed the trigger again, but the slide on his gun was locked back–he was out of ammo.

The bandit held a knife in hand, forcing Davis to drop his gun and draw his own knife. He dodged one swing, grabbing his enemy's shoulder and slashing at him. Despite being stabbed, the pirate knocked the knife out of Davis's hand and pushed him into the side of the van.

Using one hand, Davis pushed the bandit's arm away as the knife got ever closer.

"Haha, I'm gonna skin you and that girl you're with!" the bandit mocked him.

"Fuck... you!" Davis managed to whisper as he strained against the pressure.

As the knife got closer, Davis prepared for the impact. That was, however, until a gunshot left the man on the pavement, a hole in his head.

Davis turned to look at Ava, who was holding a deceased rebel's pistol.

"You good!?" she called.

"Yeah, nice shot!" Davis congratulated her. He grabbed his pistol, loading a new magazine into it as he rejoined the fight.

The windshield on Dennis's truck was gone now, having been shot with too many rounds. Brown and Matthews were firing out from inside the truck, not even bothering to lean out the windows anymore. Jackson, in the front seat, shot at them with a SIG pistol that he had.

Another helicopter, not Badger Niner Niner's, flew overhead. He was flying directly at the convoy, and the pilot began dropping bombs on the blockade.

All of the pirates were dead now, but the helicopter was a new problem. The members of 412 watched as it spun around for another pass, readying its weapons.

"Badger Niner Niner, engage that chopper!" Dennis ordered over the radio.

"Yes sir," he said, locking onto and firing at the helicopter. The rounds blasted through the glass, hitting the pilot. As the helicopter spun out of control, it eventually slammed into the ground and went up in a ball of flames.

"Good shit, Niner Niner! Let's keep moving!" Davis went on over the radio. The Convoy continued, weaving through the burning wreckage of vehicles that had been blown out of the way. They were continuing East on I-66, ready to get to Washington.

Act 2, Chapter 10 - Arlington, Virginia

Just as Badger Niner Niner had told them, the city across the river was lit up in the night sky like it would be any time outside of the apocalypse. Arlington, however, had been left to rot. Infected citizens roamed the streets. The convoy moved through the city until they reached the bridge that crossed the Potomac River.

"This is it," Davis told everyone, "Washington D.C."

Immediately as they got to the bridge, however, a black SUV with red and blue lights stopped them. A group of men wearing biohazard suits jumped out, M4 Carbine Rifles in hand.

"The city is closed to outsiders. Turn around, now!" one of them ordered, his voice muffled by the mask.

"We aren't outsiders," Davis said, stepping out of the van.

"They're Williams's boys," another of the soldiers said.

"Do we let them through?" the other asked.

"We let the last group of 'em through," the first one reasoned.

"Let's just contact Williams," another said, grabbing his radio.

"Hey, Williams is a busy man! He doesn't need you all bothering him. You know who we are, let us through!" Davis barked at the men. He flashed his government agent ID card at them, demanding to be let through.

"Yes sir, we're sorry sir," the soldier began. They got back in their SUV and pulled out of the way, letting the men back into the Capital City.

"Where we headed, Davis?" Dennis asked over the radio.

"The Pentagon. That slimy little bastard will be holed up in the Department of Defense," Davis ordered.

Act 3 - The Capital City

Act 3 Characters:

Capital Soldiers: All black uniforms, military tactical vests, gas masks. Some wear biohazard suits. All of them use M4 Carbines or Glock 17s.

Mr. President: An old white man, close to 80 years old. He wears a black suit, white shirt, and red tie.

Agent Lopez: A Mexican-American 31 year old man. Wears a gray suit with a white shirt and black tie. Has slick-back hair and carries a Glock 17.

Agent Moore: White 29 year old man. Gray suit, black shirt, gray tie. Has short hair and carries a Glock 17

Agent Anderson: Black-White mixed 34 year old man. Gray suit, white shirt, gray tie. Carries a Glock 17.

Agent Taylor: White 28 year old man. Gray suit, gray shirt, black tie. Has lengthy hair and carries a Glock 17.

Act 3, Chapter 1 - The Pentagon

The convoy proceeded to head through the streets of Washington D.C. before looping back towards the Potomac River. The convoy headed across the bridge again, ordering another group of soldiers out of their way. While most of Arlington had been abandoned, the area surrounding the Pentagon, known as Pentagon City, was protected the way D.C. was.

In the building's parking lot, multiple Black SUVs similar to the ones on the bridges, sat around. A group of soldiers jumped out of one, approaching Ava's van and Dennis's truck.

"Stop! State your name and reason for being here," the soldier demanded.

"My name is Agent Davis, and I'm here to speak to Oliver Williams."

The soldier grabbed a radio on his shoulder, beginning to speak into it.

"Williams, one of your men is here, says his name is Davis."

"I'll be right out," Williams said back over the radio.

"Wait here until you're cleared," the soldier ordered, walking away from the convoy.

Suddenly, Williams was rapidly approaching the convoy, a look of pure fury across his face.

"What are you doing here!? What are they doing here!? Who let them in!?" Williams began, approaching every soldier he saw on his way to the vehicles.

"Why are you here!?" he yelled, coming face to face with Davis.

"I'll do you one better, why *shouldn't* we be here!?" Davis asked.

"There's a reason I stopped the chopper from picking you all up!" Williams shouted.

"Oh yeah? I'd love to hear it!" Davis responded. Matthews and Brown had now gotten out of the truck and approached Williams.

"When I heard that Miller had been infected, I knew that all of you were a hazard. You all could be potentially contaminated, and I was trying my damndest to keep that shit out of the Capital!" Williams explained.

"Fuck that! This shit has burrowed into the ground and infected every city with a population over a hundred. Give me the real fucking reason," Davis said stepping forward.

There was a long period of silence as the two stared into each other's eyes.

"I'm not doing this. Not here, not now! Get out of here, while you still can!" Williams shouted at them. He turned and headed back for the building, but not before turning to one of his soldiers.

"Give them five minutes to leave, and then you have execute authority," he commanded the soldier.

"Yes sir!" the man said, confirming the command.

Despite the warning, the agents did not leave the Pentagon. They continued standing outside, pushing ever closer to the five minute grace period that Williams had given them.

"What do we do, Davis?" Dennis asked him over the radio.

"We're going inside," Davis replied. He began to approach the gate that Williams had gone through, but a crowd of soldiers surrounded him, forcing him to stop.

"Back up! You are not permitted! Leave the Premises!" they shouted. Then, one of them caught a fist to the face. It happened like a flash of lightning, the whole group of soldiers whipping out collapsable batons in unison.

Matthews and Brown ran up, pulling soldiers away from Davis. Levi also ran in, his pistol drawn. When a baton struck Brown, Levi fired a round into the crowd.

A soldier went down, prompting the remaining group to draw their firearms.

"Shit, move! Fall back!" Davis called out. The four of them scrambled for the vehicles to use as cover as the soldiers opened fire. Brown and Matthews jumped back into Dennis's truck. Levi and Davis ended up in Ava's van. Within seconds, the vehicles were pulling out of the Pentagon's parking lot and heading deeper into Washington.

Act 3, Chapter 2 - The National Mall

"Where are we going!?" Rodriguez asked over the radio, tailing the group.

"Away from the Pentagon! Away from them!" Davis informed him.

"You guys aren't gonna like what I'm seeing," Badger Niner Niner began.

"What is it?" Brown asked.

"Maybe a dozen Capital SUVs headed your way, permission to engage?" Badger stated, following with his question.

"Permission granted, give 'em hell," Davis allowed. Badger Niner Niner opened up, Forty Millimeter shells being dropped on the vehicles as they sped down the street.

A series of explosions began, but some of the vehicles swerved around the bombs. One of the vehicles caught up to Rodriguez's Humvee, swerving into it and pit-maneuvering him off the road. He skidded down a hill before hitting a marble wall, tumbling over it. The crash was followed by a splash of water, and Rodriguez coming in over the radio.

"I'm sinking!" he shouted.

"We're coming! Roll down a window!" Davis began. The other vehicles swerved off the road, stopping at the top of the hill.

Davis jumped out of the van, running down to the body of water.

"Holy shit, you crashed into the reflecting pool!" Davis shouted. Rodriguez was pulling himself out of a window on the truck, swimming away from the drowned vehicle.

"Stop! Raise your hands above your head and get down on your knees!" a soldier shouted as Rodriguez pulled himself out of the pool.

"Fuck you!" Matthews shouted, drawing his Glock 17 and firing a round through the soldier's head. The other soldiers began firing again, the group ducking behind some trees.

"You just had to shoot the bastard, huh?" Davis barked at Matthews as he fired back at the soldiers.

"What, you wanted to get arrested?" Matthews retorted.

"We need to fall back! Head towards the Lincoln Memorial!" Rodriguez ordered the group. He darted from one tree to the next, heading up the pool towards the monument.

"We should go the other way! Towards the Washington Monument!" Matthews objected.

"That's a wide open field, they'd have easy shots on us there!"

"Exactly, so they wouldn't *expect* us to go that way!" Matthews continued.

"No, we're going to the Memorial!" Davis said, backing Rodriguez up. The group began following the rebels to the memorial, hiding behind trees and laying down cover fire for each other. When they finally reached the stairs up to the memorial, it was littered with abandoned food vendor carts and water bottles.

"Inside!" Rodriguez ordered.

Doing as he said, the agents followed inside as the rebels flooded the room.

But that was their downfall.

Bullets began flying as Capital Soldiers jumped out from behind the pillars in the monument.

"Shit!" Rodriguez shouted as he shot one down. A bullet whisked past Davis's head, slamming into Matthews's soldier.

"I'm hit!" Matthews shouted. Another round came from behind him, striking him in the thigh. As he stumbled forward, he fell to the ground.

Davis and Brown fired down several more soldiers, Brown rushing to Matthews's side.

"Shit, help me stop the bleeding!" Brown shouted. Davis ran over, putting pressure on his thigh as Brown put pressure on his shoulder.

"I can't stop it, there's an entry and an exit!" Davis shouted. As the last soldier in the room went down, Rodriguez joined at Matthews's side.

"I should've listened to him! We should've gone to the fuckin' Monument," Davis shouted, his hands soaked in blood.

"There's no way we could've known that they were setting us up here," Rodriguez defended.

"I knew," Matthews managed to whisper, his eyes staring at the marble ceiling.

"Shit, they hit his femoral artery... we can't do anything!" Davis shouted, assessing the blood loss. Now, the soldiers that had been chasing them were beginning to come up the stairs.

"Cover me, I'm carrying him out of here!" Davis commanded, pulling Matthews over his shoulder and drawing his Glock.

"We've got you, move!" Brown shouted to him.

Bullets began flying, soldiers dying on the stairs. The white marble was stained red, tainted by the violence and betrayal that these men had brought into the country. Under Williams's orders, the men gave their lives for a dishonorable cause.

Now, Matthews was bleeding out on Davis's shoulder. He'd been failed. Not only by his men, but his country. His commanders. Left to die because of their mistake.

"Keep going!" Davis shouted, his ears ringing. He felt lightheaded, the feeling of dread flooding through his body. He couldn't stop blaming himself.

I failed him. I got him killed.

The thoughts wouldn't stop.

A group of soldiers rushed over, but were met by a different group.

"Fall back! There's been a breach at the Arlington Bridge!" one of the soldiers shouted. The soldiers turned and ran, some of them still firing as they ran backwards. Those soldiers didn't make it far as a speeding minivan slammed into them.

"Ava!" Davis shouted, heading for the doors.

"Get in! Put him in the back!" Ava shouted, rolling her window down.

Levi jumped in the passenger seat while Brown and Davis climbed into the back, laying Matthews down across the seat. Rodriguez and his men jumped in the back hatch, firing at the fleeing soldiers as Ava pulled away.

"What happened!?" Ava asked, looking at Matthews in the rearview.

"They jumped us in the Goddamn Lincoln Memorial," Davis shouted, staring at Matthews. Despite their best efforts, he was lost. His eyes stared up at the car ceiling, just as they had in the Memorial. His chest rising and falling with his panicked breaths had ceased. He was unmoving. Brown touched a hand to his arm, but his skin was cold. Both of the men sat staring, soaked in their brother's blood.

"First Miller, now Matthews..." Brown began, but he lost himself before he could finish the thought.

"Ava, head for the bridge into Arlington," Davis told her, turning around.

"What for?"

"That's where the bastards who did this are going."

Act 3, Chapter 3 - Arlington Memorial Bridge

The van pulled up to the bridge that they'd crossed only hours ago. On the bridge, dozens of Military SUVs blocked the agents' sightlines.

"They said there was a breach, what do you think breached the defenses?" Brown asked.

"We're about to find out," Levi began.

"Davis, this is Dennis. Come in!" a voice called over the radio.

"Go ahead Dennis," Davis answered.

"We're taking heavy fire at the Washington Monument. Where are you guys?" Dennis asked.

"We're at the Arlington Bridge! Is Niner Niner with you?" Davis radioed.

"Yeah, he's doing his best to cover us!" Dennis continued.

"Just hold them off til we're done here!" Davis ordered Badger Niner Niner.

"Copy that," Badger responded.

Ava stopped the van, looking out over the bridge. Past the vehicles, hundreds of infected citizens marched across it. The soldiers were in front of their SUVs, firing as many rounds as they could towards the crowd.

"Watch this shit," Davis began, jumping out of the van with a gas can in his hand.

"What is he doing!?" Levi asked, watching.

His question was answered as Davis began pouring the gas in a line behind the SUVs. When he was done, he threw the gas can on the ground next to the end of the line.

With that, he pulled a match box out of his pocket. There were only three matches left in it, so he grabbed one.

He struck the match, tossing it at the far end of the gasoline line. He quickly ran back to the van as Ava put it in reverse, getting away from the fuse as fast as possible.

"Holy shit, you're crazy!" Brown shouted. The line ignited from one end to the other, reaching the can at the end.

A flash of light covered the bridge as the explosion set one vehicle ablaze.

A chain reaction blew from one side of the bridge to the other, the opposite direction of where the fire had started.

"Good luck keeping this infection out of D.C. now, asshole," Davis scoffed, mocking Williams.

Act 3, Chapter 4 - Washington Monument

"We're still taking heavy fire, are you on your way yet!?"

Dennis begged over the radio. The sound of Johnson and Jackson giving gunfire in return echoed through the radio.

"We're headed your way!" Davis responded.

When they reached the monument, several SUVs covered the grassy area. Dennis, Jackson, and Johnson took cover behind the pillar, occasionally peeking out to fire at their enemies.

In the sky, Badger Niner Niner was firing down at the hostiles, but most of the soldiers were able to get out of the way before the projectiles hit them.

"Move behind them!" Davis told Ava, pointing to the attackers.

Doing as he told her, she moved them behind the soldiers as they approached the monument. Brown and Davis jumped out, firing at the soldiers from behind. The soldiers that they didn't hit turned to look at where the bullets were coming from, giving Dennis a chance to jump out and shoot the rest down.

"I think we're clear!" Jackson shouted, stepping out. Just then a round flew by his head, missing him by less than an inch. However, it didn't miss its target.

"Shit!" Jackson shouted, turning to his brother. Johnson had taken a round, straight to the chest. The agents, Jackson, and Dennis all rushed to his side, holding him.

"Holy fuck! What do we do!?" Jackson shouted.

"That's a heart shot... there's nothing we *can* do," Davis began.

Johnson exhaled, a whisper leaving his lips.

"Behind you," he mumbled. Davis and Brown turned around as the soldier fired another round. This one hit Johnson square in the forehead, leaving a stream of blood down the bridge of his nose and onto his cheek.

"Fuck!" Jackson shouted, drawing his pistol and firing all twelve rounds into the soldier's chest.

He reloaded the gun, firing three more into the soldier's head.

"What do we do!?" Jackson shouted. He got to his feet and took a few steps back before his knees gave out again, and he fell onto them.

"We outta bury him," Dennis began.

"There's no time," Levi said, pointing towards a crowd of infected citizens that was following the sound of gunshots.

"Where are my men?" Rodriguez asked.

"They went towards the White House. They figured the president would be able to do something about Williams," Dennis answered.

"Then we're going to the White House," Rodriguez ordered.

Act 3, Chapter 5 - The White House

A helicopter hovered overhead, firing machine guns at a group of rebels that were hiding behind a checkpoint wall. They'd breached the fence, and had begun up the driveway to the presidential office.

"Get away from the fucking White House!" a voice yelled over the chopper's intercom.

"Fuck you!" a rebel shouted back, firing his rifle at the Helicopter's underbelly.

The chopper fired back, but the rebel's cover stopped the rounds from hitting him. Secret Service agents flooded out of the building, firing rounds at the rebels. That's when Dennis's truck pulled up, the agents firing from the back of it. Rodriguez also stood in the back, popping rounds off from his Colt Python.

No secret service agents stood between the rebels and the White House, other than the helicopter. Brown turned his M4 at the helicopter's tail propeller, firing a burst of rounds at it.

Almost immediately, the chopper began spinning out of control and slammed into the fence around the White House, taking it down and skidding into the street where it promptly exploded.

"Move in!" Rodriguez yelled to his men. Meeting at the door, the rebel strike team and the members of 412 made it to the building. Davis kicked the door in, allowing the men to enter.

Inside they began taking fire from more secret service agents, forcing them to dive into side rooms. A rebel fired his pistol, taking out one secret service agent as he ran down the hallway.

"Don't stop moving!" Rodriguez ordered. The rebels began moving again as the agents gave them cover fire. They eventually reached the door to the Oval Office, one of them kicking the door in as the agents executed the rest of the secret service agents.

"Holy shit! Don't kill me!" the president called from inside as he was surrounded by rebels.

"We want to talk about Williams," one of them said. The rest of 412 and Rodriguez ran into the office, facing the POTUS.

"Williams!? What about him!?" the president asked, taking a step back.

"Why'd he leave us in West Virginia!? Let's start with that!" Davis barked.

"Miller was compromised, all of you were compromised! We couldn't risk bringing the infection back to the Capital, but that doesn't matter much anymore," said the President.

"Why did he order his men to kill us?" Brown asked next.

"That one is obvious! You men are vengeful, spiteful, and bloodthirsty. If we just let you back into the Capital you would've burned it to the ground in seconds!"

"How did you know that Miller was compromised?" Davis asked, his voice more toned down now.

"What?"

"How did you know that Miller got infected!?"

"You radioed it in!"

"No... we didn't," Brown said, stepping up.

"It was their fucking *plan* to leave us behind!" Davis shouted.

"Okay, fine! We had men surveying you all, we knew every move you made in that town. As soon as you were dispatched, Unit 413 was formed to make sure your objective was complete or you were killed!"

"Unit 413?" Davis asked.

"Commander Williams's newest Task Unit. I gave him the authority to make it without your knowledge," the president admitted.

"What do we do with this *viejo gringo andrajoso*?" Rodrigeuz asked.

"We're taking him with us," Davis said, grabbing the president.

"For what?" Brown asked.

"So he can order Williams to stop this bullshit," Davis answered, marching out the door with him. The walk was short lived, however, because a massive tentacle sprung up through the ground.

"Shit!" Davis shouted, dropping the president. The biomass had spread under the White House, and was protruding through the fountain in the yard.

"Look out!" Brown shouted as the tentacle grabbed the president.

"Cut him out!" Davis shouted, drawing his knife. He began sawing through the tentacle, blood splattering everywhere.

Brown did the same, cutting from the other side. When they met in the middle, the tentacle fell and released the president. But it was too late. As the man rose to his feet, he turned around in shambles. His eyes were bloodshot and his skin was a sickly pale color.

"Shit, the president is infected! *¡Qué asombroso!*" Rodriguez shouted.

"What the hell do we do about this!?" a rebel asked.

"Kill the *hijo de puta*!" Rodriguez ordered. A rebel pulled a gun and fired one round through the infected president's head, causing him to fall limp onto the ground.

"This shit has gotten out of hand. We need to get back to Williams," Davis stated.

Act 3, Chapter 6 - Unit 413

But the agents didn't even make it off the property before an SUV pulled up. Four men jumped out, wearing gray suits.

"These are the same clowns that hopped off the chopper in Moorefield!" Rodriguez pointed out.

"Who are you!?" Davis called out to them, Matthews's rifle clutched in his hands.

"My name is Agent Moore with Unit 413. This is Anderson, Taylor, and Lopez. In the name of the United States of America, and Commander Oliver Williams, you are under arrest!" one of them called out.

"I wouldn't recommend getting in our way, *amigo*," Rodriguez called out to them.

"I wouldn't recommend telling us what to do, *gilipollas*," Agent Lopez called back to him.

"Alright, that's enough," Rodriguez growled, pulling his revolver from his holster and pointing it at the agent. The agents took cover as he pulled the trigger, the round ending up lodged in the SUV door. The agents began firing back, rounds slamming into the sides of Dennis's truck as they climbed into it.

"Get us out of here!" Davis ordered.

Dennis took off, hitting the gas as the rounds hit the sides. Seconds later, the SUV took off in pursuit after them.

"Stop them!" Davis ordered Brown, who was looking back at them. Jackson and Brown leaned out the windows, firing at the driver with their sidearms.

"Shit, brace yourselves!" Dennis called back to the others as a round slammed into his tire.

The truck skidded off the road, hitting a pole. The pole fell over, landing on top of the truck as it stopped. Just then, Ava's van pulled up alongside them. Levi jumped out of it, firing at the SUV as it sped towards them.

"Hop in, quick!" Ava told them. The group jumped out of the truck, getting in the van. As they sped away from the truck, the SUV continued pursuing them.

"My truck! We need to go back for my truck!" Dennis cried.

"We need to shake these guys first!" Davis said, firing a round out the window. Ava skidded around a corner, clutching the handbrake as she rounded it.

"Woo, you're pretty good at this!" Davis cheered her on, looking out the window again. A stray round took out Ava's side view mirror.

"Aim for their tires!" Rodriguez said, firing his Python out the window. One round, unclear who's weapon it was fired from, did hit the front right tire, sending the SUV through the window of a clothing store.

"Now, back for my truck!" Dennis said. Obediently, Ava rounded the corner and headed back for where Dennis had crashed.

Dennis got in the truck, turning his key in the ignition as he pulled away from the pole. It left a sizable dent in his roof, which caused him to punch the dashboard a few times before getting away from the pole.

"Fuck!" Dennis said, stepping out of the truck and slamming the door behind him. He turned to Davis, who was approaching him.

"You got a light?" Dennis asked, flicking a lighter several times under a cigarette. The lighter didn't produce a flame, causing him to toss it away.

"Here you go," Davis said, pulling out his match box. He struck one match, holding it up to Dennis's cigarette.

"Thanks," Dennis responded, taking a hit of the cigarette. A second passed before he sniffed the air, looking around.

"Do you smell something?" Dennis asked, looking at the others. Then, he noticed the gasoline puddle pouring out of his tank.

"Shit, the glue didn't hold!" he shouted, bending down to look at it.

"Dennis, your cigarette!" Brown shouted, but it was too late. The fumes were ignited, and Dennis lit ablaze.

"Holy shit!" Davis shouted. He took a step forward but Levi put a hand on his chest and pushed him back. All of them fell to the ground as the gas tank ignited, blowing the truck apart.

"Dennis!" Jackson shouted, approaching the charred remains.

"Fuck! We're dropping like flies!" Brown shouted, taking a step back.

Act 3, Chapter 7 - March on the Pentagon

"We're going back," Davis said, pulling himself into Ava's van and shutting the door.

"Back where?" Ava asked.

"The Pentagon, we're gonna kill that asshole Williams this time," Davis explained.

"Okay, let's go then," she said as Levi, Brown, Jackson, and Rodriguez got in the van. She shifted the van into drive and pulled away from the scene.

"All members of Unit 412, this is Agent Davis. We're moving on the Pentagon," Davis began through the radio.

"Copy that Davis, moving your way," Badger Niner Niner said over the radio. Before Davis knew it, multiple rebel trucks were following Ava's van. The attack helicopter flew overhead, Badger Niner Niner looking down on the others.

"Let's go fuck this guy up," Brown said, loading a new magazine into his pistol.

**

The vehicles were lined up in front of the Pentagon now, but there was heavy resistance. Where there were once dozens of Military SUVs, there were now hundreds. Capital soldiers flooded the parking lot, weapons drawn and pointed at the convoy.

"Stand down or we will open fire!" someone called through a megaphone.

"We are going to kill you all if you don't get out of our *fucking* way!" Badger called through his radio.

Another helicopter took off from the Pentagon, meeting Niner Niner in the air.

"Shit," he began over the radio, "I have to deal with the chopper, can you cover the ground?"

"We've got you, take that bird out of the sky," Davis said.

"Sergeant Wilson, can I trust you not to shoot me in the back," Rodriguez asked, handing him a gun.

"I'd choose to shoot any of these government assholes before I shot you any day," Wilson said, taking the gun.

"You are outnumbered!" a voice called through the megaphone again.

"That might be true," Davis began, climbing on top of Ava's van, "But we aren't a bunch of sheep, listening to what the 'man in charge' tells us to do!"

"Stand down, now!" the megaphone repeated.

Davis turned to Ava, who was standing next to the driver's side door of the van.

"Hey, if we make it out of here," Davis said.

"*When* we make it out of here," Ava corrected.

"Right... *when* we make it out of here, I'd like to get to know you better. Maybe grab a drink sometime?" Davis asked.

"If you can find a bar that's still open after all this, sure. I'd love to have a drink with you, Agent Davis," Ava said, a grin on her face.

"What will it be!?" the voice on the megaphone asked.

"Badger Niner Niner," Davis began on his radio.

"Go ahead, Davis."

"Fuck 'em up."

With that, the chopper opened fire on the other, circling around in the air to avoid the return fire.

"Open fire!" the soldier shouted into the megaphone. The Capital soldiers began shooting at the convoy, everybody running for cover as the bullets bounced off the sides of the vehicles.

"Levi, where are you!?" Davis called into his radio. He had lost sight of him as soon as the bullets had started flying. Rounds soaring through the air overhead, Davis ducked between cars looking for his men.

"Levi!?" he called. He rounded the corner of a vehicle, where Levi was being held by the shoulders, struggling against a blade that was being pushed towards his chest.

"Levi!" Davis shouted, drawing his pistol and shooting the soldier that was trying to kill him.

"Thanks, I thought I was gonna–" Levi began, but was interrupted by a gunshot that ripped through his skull, the bullet almost hitting Davis as well.

"Holy shit!" Davis shouted, ducking back into cover. Levi was gone, that was a kill shot.

"Guys, I lost Levi," Davis began over his radio.

"Lost him?" someone asked.

"Headshot, he's gone," Davis said, his voice breaking.

"Shit, we've got to keep moving!" Rodriguez said. The helicopters continued flying around each other, exchanging volleys of rounds. Badger Niner Niner dodged some bullets, but others hit the hull of his chopper.

"We need to take them out!" Brown shouted, firing at the soldiers. One of the rounds from the helicopters fell on some of the SUVs, blowing them up.

"Hell yeah! More of that, Badger!" Rodriguez called into the radio. The ground troops began pushing towards the Pentagon, gunning down the soldiers in their way.

As soon as they made it to the line that had been set up, Badger Niner Niner managed to take down the enemy helicopter, sending it spinning out of control into the building.

“Enemy chopper down,” Badger said into his radio.

“Copy that, we’re entering the Pentagon,” Davis responded. He turned to Ava, who was standing behind him.

“You wait out here, we’ll be back,” he told her. Then, he turned to the building’s door and kicked it in, breaching into the Pentagon.

Inside, a long hallway stood in front of them. The fluorescent lights revealed several Capital soldiers with guns pointed at the door.

“Contact!” Davis shouted, firing at one and diving into a room. Brown followed him, while Rodriguez and Jackson went the other way. The soldiers began moving up through the hallway, giving the members of 412 open shots on them.

“Now!” Davis ordered, Brown and Rodriguez peeking out of their room and shooting the enemies down.

“Let’s move!”

They began down the hallway, passing the soldiers they’d gunned down. They got to another door, kicking it in. Inside, dozens of computer terminals sat turned on with soldiers using them as cover.

“They’re here!” one shouted, opening fire on the group.

“Where’s that bastard Williams!?” Davis shouted, shooting one soldier down. Within seconds, the entire group of soldiers in the room was down. All except for the agents of Unit 413, who ran into the room, their weapons drawn.

Anderson turned to the others, talking to them.

“Go find Williams, tell him they’re here,” he commanded them. Obediently, they turned and ran out from the room to go to Williams.

“Come on out, Davis!” Anderson called, beginning to walk into the room. He held his Glock 17 in his hand, scanning the room for movement.

"I promise things will end up better if you come with me... willingly," he shouted.

"Tell me where Williams is, asshole!" Davis shouted. Anderson turned in the direction that the words came from, starting to walk towards them.

"Come with me and you'll find out."

"Maybe you should just tell me and save us the trouble!" Davis called out again. This time, his voice carried from the other side of the room. Anderson turned, confused.

"Where are you!? Show yourself!" he snapped, losing his patience.

"Come and find me, asshat!" Davis called back. Anderson couldn't distinguish what part of the room his voice was coming from.

"We already got Matthews! Your friend outside, and the truck driver! The quiet one at the Washington Monument! You're all going down, whether you like it or not," Anderson mocked.

"That might be, but you're going down first!" Davis shouted, springing on Anderson from behind. He slammed him in the back of the head with a chair, which knocked Anderson to the ground. He quickly drew his pistol, pointing it at the agent.

"Look out!" Brown called to Davis. Anderson had also pulled his pistol, pointing it at Davis. He dodged to the side as the round went off, whisking past his head.

He jumped into cover, firing some rounds at Anderson. All of the rounds missed, except one that grazed his shoulder. Davis peeked back up as Anderson stumbled back from the pain, firing another round into his stomach.

The force knocked him back, causing him to fall down. Davis jumped out and approached him.

"Where is Williams!?" Davis barked at him.

"Fuck you!" Anderson responded.

"Tell me!" Davis shouted, pointing the gun at Anderson.

"Lean in," Anderson said with a grin.

"Fuck that, tell me!"

"I'm bleeding out here, man, I can't talk loudly... lean in."

Davis gave in, leaning in to hear what Anderson had to say.

"Now!" Anderson shouted, falling back from his elbows onto his back as a group of Capital soldiers ran into the room.

"Shit, take cover!" Davis shouted.

All of the members ducked back behind the terminals. Davis shot one soldier, but Anderson sprung to his feet and tackled him.

"What happened to bleeding out," Davis asked, struggling.

"Bullet proof vest, something Williams never gave you pricks," Anderson said, ripping his shirt open to reveal the kevlar vest underneath.

Anderson pulled the knife that Davis had tucked in his pocket, flipping it open and beginning to press it towards him.

"Shit! Help!" Davis shouted as the others shot down the breaching soldiers. He pushed against Anderson's arms, keeping the knife away from himself. Shots continued ringing out through the room, Davis losing his grip.

He watched as Jackson took a round, going down onto the floor. He couldn't help, but he felt awful anyway. Bullet casings covered the floor as the gunfight continued, Davis barely resisting Anderson's attack. Just then, a single round passed through Anderson's head, leaving him to slump down onto the floor.

Behind him, Ava stood with Anderson's Glock 17, the barrel smoking.

"I thought I told you to–wait outside," Davis began, pulling himself to his feet.

"Well, I can't get a drink with a corpse, so I figured I'd help," Ava laughed.

"Where's Williams?" she asked, turning to him as Brown shot down the last soldier.

"Good question."

Act 3, Chapter 8 - Searching the Pentagon

The group left the terminal room, heading for the East side of the building.

"Where are we going?" Rodriguez asked.

"No idea, but I'm going to search every inch of this building until we find this fucker," Davis responded. Brown was carrying Jackson on his shoulder, who had been shot in the gunfight.

"How's he doing?" Davis asked.

"Not well, he passed out when he fell but he still has a pulse," Brown answered.

The group turned down a different hallway, continuing towards the East side of the building. A group of Capital soldiers jumped out, weapons in hand.

"Stop right there!" one of them shouted. There was no cover to get behind, so Davis threw his hands up and took a step back.

"Don't move!" another soldier yelled.

"Okay, calm down," Davis said, his hands above his head.

"Shut your fucking mouth!" the soldier yelled back, his gun still pointed at the Agent.

"Williams, this is the East Side patrol. We've got 412 in custody," he said into his radio.

A voice came over the radio, but Davis couldn't understand what he said.

"Yes sir," he said. He then looked back at the rest of his soldiers before looking back at Davis.

"You heard him. Kill 'em."

A second later, Sergeant Wilson burst through a door behind the soldiers, Rodriguez's gun in hand.

He fired two rounds into one's back, moving the barrel to the next and firing a few more. Within five seconds, the room was clear of soldiers.

That was, until, another soldier jumped out from a side room and grabbed Wilson. In his hand, he clutched a knife that he pressed against the officer's throat.

"Drop the gun!" the soldier's voice pierced Wilson's ears. Obediently, he tossed the gun to the side. The soldier's eyes focused on the men at the other end of the hallway, now.

"None of you move, or I swear to God I'll slit his throat!" he shouted.

"We're not moving," Davis said, compliantly. However, he was slowly inching his hand towards his waistband where his pistol was tucked.

"I see that hand moving! Stop!" the soldier shouted.

"Sir, I'm not moving," Davis continued, lying.

"I'll kill this little rat, I swear!" the soldier went on. Davis raised his hands back up, trying to calm the man down. But it was too late. With a quick pulling motion, red mist sprayed across the hall, painting the white walls crimson.

"No!" Davis shouted, drawing his pistol and firing three rounds into the soldier as the officer's body dropped to the floor. The men moved down the hallway, Rodriguez stopping at Wilson's corpse.

"It was an honor working with you, *sargento*," he said, grabbing his gun from the floor.

"Wait," someone said. They turned to Brown, but he hadn't said it. Jackson, still in Brown's arms, was gasping.

"Put me down," Jackson gasped out.

Brown did so, setting him gently against the wall. Jackson was bleeding heavily, his exhales raspy and wheezy.

"What is it?" Davis asked, kneeling down next to him.

"I'm not gonna make it out of this building, and you can't haul me around the whole damn place," Jackson said.

"We aren't leaving you. Brown, pick him back up," Davis began.

"No, you have to leave me. Brown ain't gon' be able to carry me everywhere. I'm done for," Jackson muttered.

"We won't forget you, *compadre,*" Rodriguez said, laying a hand on Jackson's shoulder.

Only the four of them left, Davis, Rodriguez, Ava, and Brown continued into the hallway. There was another room full of terminals, in which several Capital soldiers jumped out from behind. Without even blinking, Davis drew his gun and shot all of them down in seconds.

There was one soldier left, which Davis shot in the arm. The shot caused the man to drop his gun, but Davis shot him in the leg anyway.

"Tell me where Williams is, and I'll consider letting you live," Davis threatened, bending down to face the soldier he'd wounded.

"Out there!" the soldier cried, pointing at a window on the back wall. Davis looked out, seeing a small three story building about fifty yards from the side of the Pentagon. One light was on, shining through a window on the top floor.

"What is he doing in there!?" Davis asked, turning back to the soldier.

"I have no idea, he wouldn't tell any of us! He wouldn't even tell 413!" the soldier begged.

"We're getting into that building, let's go!" Davis said, popping a round in the soldier's head and shattering his promise.

Act 3, Chapter 9 - Into the Factory

The group found a doorway on the East side of the building.

Davis pushed against it, but it was locked. He took a deep breath before

stepping back.

"Brown, take this fucking door off it's hinges."

He stepped back before charging up a kick that knocked the door open. The top hinge snapped off the doorframe, leaving it hanging from the wall.

"Let's go!" he said. The group began out of the building and through the lot. However, the thousands of infected citizens that they'd allowed into the Capital from the Arlington bridge had arrived, and were marching their way through the Pentagon's parking lot. Davis darted to the entrance to the building.

"Badger Niner Niner, do you have eyes on me?" he asked into the radio.

"Copy, I see you, Davis," Niner Niner responded.

"Scan this building we're going into," Davis ordered.

"Copy that, pulling schematics," he began.

Davis opened the door to the building, revealing an empty warehouse. There were some larger machines, but their uses were unclear.

"Keep moving," Davis said.

"You see anybody?" Brown asked.

"No, do you?" Davis answered, responding with his own question.

"Oddly enough... No, I don't," Brown answered.

In that second, bullets pinged off the machinery around them, flashes of light coming from a balcony above them.

"Shit, look up!" Rodriguez shouted. He ran for cover, but never made it. A round hit him in the side of the leg, dropping him to one knee.

"Rodriguez!" Brown shouted. The soldiers on the balcony didn't stop, however, littering the rebel leader with rounds as they blasted him to Hell.

"You fuckers are gonna pay for that!" Brown shouted.

"Find the stairs!" Davis ordered. Brown began looking around, peeking out of cover slightly to find a staircase.

"I see them, this side!" Brown called from the right side of the room. Davis began firing his pistol at the soldiers on the balcony, moving from cover to cover.

"Ava, behind us!" he ordered her, beginning up the stairs.

"Davis, this is Badger Niner Niner. The room Williams is in will be inaccessible from that balcony. There should be a second staircase somewhere downstairs that will take you to the third floor."

"Copy that, thanks for the help," Davis said over the radio.

He made his way up the stairs, shooting at the few soldiers that remained up there. When they were clear, Ava continued up the stairs behind them.

"I got you all now!" someone shouted from downstairs.

One single gunshot rang out through the building.

One gunshot caused Davis's face to go pale.

One gunshot caused Davis's blood to run cold.

One. Single. Gunshot.

Ava fell forward, barely catching herself as she landed. Brown quickly turned around and fired a burst of three rounds into the soldier at the bottom of the stairs.

Davis was frozen. Time was a blur, and his vision was moving in and out of focus. His ears were ringing as he stared at the girl laying on the floor.

"She's still breathing!" Brown shouted, picking her up, but his words hit Davis like he was speaking in slow motion. Davis was snapped out of his hypnosis by Badger Niner Niner's voice on the radio.

"I've got eyes on Williams through that window! He's working on some sort of computer terminal!"

Act 3, Chapter 10 - Cold Hard Facts

"Copy that, Badger," Davis said into his microphone. As they got to the bottom of the stairs, Badger Niner Niner's voice carried over the radio again.

"Rodriguez, you've got men outside being crowded by this horde," he said.

"Rodriguez is down, you're gonna have to help them!" Davis told the pilot.

They continued searching until Davis finally found a door behind one of the machines, a staircase to the top floor stretching behind it.

"Over here!" Davis called to Brown, who walked over with Ava's body still on his shoulders.

"How's she doing?" Davis asked.

"I'm not sure," Brown responded. With the opportunity to march up those stairs and kill the man responsible for all this, but the choice to stay down here with the woman he loved, Davis grabbed her off of Brown's shoulders.

He placed her on the ground, staring into her eyes.

"I'm getting cold, Davis," she said, glancing at him.

"You're gonna be okay," Davis reassured her, but did not convince himself.

"Do me a favor... After you kill that asshole, go have that drink for me," Ava said, "Have two. One for me, one for you."

"I will," Davis began, his voice shaking.

"Davis, you ready?" Brown asked.

"Just another minute, okay?" Davis asked, tears welling up in his eyes.

"You know that I don't have another minute," Ava coughed. Blood spewed out of her mouth, dripping down her lips to her chin.

There was a bang on the door that they'd breached through, and it fell from its frame. Several infected citizens, including a now infected Rodriguez, stumbled into the room, growling and frothing at the mouth.

"Go, Davis," Ava gasped.

"I love you!" Davis shouted, breaking as tears ran down his cheeks.

"I love you too, now go!" Ava responded before her eyes glossed over, staring at the ceiling, but not at the ceiling. They stared at something past the ceiling, something higher.

Davis stared into the girl's eyes, wiping his face before turning around.

"Let's go," he said, beginning up the staircase.

He reached the top, which had a large furnished living space. Sitting at a desk against one wall, Williams was typing on a computer that was plugged into several wires and cables.

Davis squeezed the trigger, a bullet piercing Williams's shoulder and knocking him out of the chair. The office chair rolled across the floor, falling over. Davis approached the man, but something else caught his eye.

Flashing on the screen that Williams had been sitting at were the words "Access Granted". A green flashing filled the room as Davis turned to Williams.

"What did you do!?" he shouted, pointing his gun at him.

"Wouldn't you like to know," Williams said, clutching his shoulder.

"Davis, keep your gun on him, I'm gonna check this out," Brown said, rushing to grab the chair and sit down at the terminal. He began typing while Davis kept aiming at Williams.

"Tell us what you did!" Davis demanded.

"He'll find out soon enough."

Brown stepped away from his chair, pointing his gun at Williams again. On the screen, the word "Downloading" was displayed over a progress bar that read "2%"

Just then, several men ran up the stairs into the room. They began firing several shots at the pair of agents, who dodged out of the way. Brown got behind a sofa, while Davis dodged into a closet.

"Give up, Davis!" Lopez's voice called out.

"Oh, look who it is! If it isn't Unit 413!" Brown shouted. He fired at a couple Capital soldiers that had breached with them. Davis peeked out of cover while they were focused on Brown, putting a bullet clean between Moore's eyes. The guns shifted to focusing on the closet, which allowed Brown to stand up and pick off Lopez.

"Look out!" Williams shouted, pointing at the sofa. The other men turned, firing a barrage of rounds into Brown while he was standing.

"Shit! No!" Davis yelled, jumping out of cover and shooting every last man he saw. Agent Taylor went down next, clutching a wound in his chest as he fell to the floor. The rest of the Capital soldiers fell around him, leaving only Davis, Brown, and Williams. Brown was heavily injured, several bullets having pierced his lower abdomen.

"Fuck! Tell me what it is!" Davis shouted, stepping out and pointing his gun at Williams.

"See for yourself," Williams said, pointing to the computer. The download had completed, and tons of words covered the screen. Most prominently was a window with an image of the machines from downstairs.

"Neurotoxin Emitters Active" the screen read. Davis took a step back from the screen, turning to Williams.

"Neurotoxins!?" he shouted.

"A more advanced form of the infection we all know and love," Williams began, "It's brilliant!"

"Brilliant!?" Davis shouted, "Fucking brilliant!?"

"When I created the first biomass, I knew it was dangerous, I knew it had to be contained," Williams began.

"You *created* the biomass!?" Davis went on, his gun trained on Williams's head.

"It was a mistake! I needed it destroyed. That's why I sent you. But you were too late, too slow. Too weak. An hour after you touched down in West Virginia, two more of those things burrowed out of the ground in surrounding areas," Williams explained.

"So instead of sending 413 to stop those, you sent them to spy on us!? And then abandoned us!?"

"I needed that sample that you collected," Williams defended.

"Well here, have it!" Davis shouted, throwing the vial at Williams's feet.

"It's too late now! I have a new plan. This country was already crumbling before I came in. Now, the world will remember America as a country that went up in a ball of flames! Died an honorable death! Not a country that shriveled up and withered away!" Williams shouted.

"Turn off the Emitters!" Davis barked at him.

"And what if I don't?" Williams asked, a smile across his face.

"Do it!" Davis shouted, pointing the gun at Williams's chest.

"You're gonna burn with me," Williams said, a smile on his face. Then, he leaned his head back and closed his eyes, falling to the floor.

He'd died from blood loss.

"Dammit!" Davis shouted, walking back to the terminal.

He began typing on it, trying to turn the Emitters off, but the words "Access Denied" flashed across the screen with a red light.

"Brown!" Davis said, approaching the agent as he laid unconscious on the floor. He shook him awake.

"Brown, I need you to do something!" Davis shouted.

"Fuck, what is it!?" Brown gasped, waking up.

"I need you to turn this off," Davis said, picking Brown up and setting him down in the chair.

"Jesus, it seems like you've been telling me what to do ever since we got off that damn chopper," Brown gasped, leaning on the keyboard.

"I know, buddy, I know. And I'm sorry, but you've got to do this or we're all fucked," Davis said, a worried look on his face.

"What is it?" Brown asked.

"Neurotoxin Emitters. A more advanced version of the infection, Brown. Brown, he made the biomass!" Davis explained.

"That bastard, we should've killed him the minute he hired us," Brown coughed. He began typing on the keyboard, but the Access Denied screen didn't go away. He loaded up a folder, which explained details about the Neurotoxin. Flashing on the screen was a message saying "Emitter Chamber Breached".

"Shit, I can't fix it," Brown began.

"Why not," Davis asked as Brown pulled himself out of the chair.

"Williams's men, they shot holes in the chambers. There's no way to seal it. It's over," Brown continued, sitting down on the floor. His white shirt had been stained red as he stared into Davis's eyes.

"It's over," he said as he exhaled for the last time.

"Fuck!" Davis shouted, standing up and moving to the terminal. He began reading the details folder, looking for a way to stop the Neurotoxin.

"Highly flammable... Highly explosive... Burns clean, no toxins emitted when burned..." he muttered, reading details.

He took a step back, pulling his matchbox out of his pocket. Empty.

"Dammit!" Davis shouted, throwing the box across the room.

"This is Agent Davis with 412, somebody come in," Davis said into his radio. Nobody responded.

"Someone come in! Please!"

"This is Badger Niner Niner, I read you loud and clear, Davis."

"Badger, you see the building off the East side of the Pentagon, three stories tall, light on in the top floor window?"

"I see it."

"Engage that building," Davis ordered.

"Sir, the scanners are marking you as danger-close to that target, are you sure?"

"Engage the damn building!"

"Copy that, engaging."

The infected from the bottom floor had made it up the stairs, and Davis began firing at them as they marched towards him. Machine gun fire could be heard pelting the outside of the building, the chopper blasting it to Hell.

Davis looked at the crowd of infected that was flooding into the room. He pressed a bookshelf against them, but they managed to push it out of the way.

Among the infected that he saw, Ava's body had reanimated and was pushing through the crowd towards him.

"Ava!" Davis shouted.

She, of course, did not respond.

Bullets began piercing the side of the building, some hitting the infected citizens. A round hit the wall, but didn't create a spark.

More bullets continued through the building, decimating the infected. One bullet hit Ava, causing her to disappear into the crowd.

"No!" Davis shouted. Suddenly, an infected hand grabbed Davis's arm, pulling him onto a leather chair. Davis stumbled back, seeing the eyes of Williams, who had transformed into one of his own creations.

"Get away from me!" Davis shouted, kicking at the infected. The bullets continued piercing through the building. One infected began tearing into Davis's stomach, but was only able to break the skin for a second before–

A round must have hit something that created a spark, as the building went up in an instant.

The building exploded outward, sending debris and infected corpses into the sky.

"Woo! Building is gone!" Badger Niner Niner began over the radio.

"Davis, target decimated. Any further orders?"

"Davis?"

In loving memory of
Mary Hart

Unit 412

J.L. Hart

(812)-610-2489

About the Author

J.L. Hart is a 17-year-old high school student who lives in Indiana. Having always had a creative mind, J.L. Hart quickly decided to dive into writing, getting their career started as quickly as their Junior year. As of now, J.L. Hart has published multiple books, including The Shadow series.

Milton Keynes UK
Ingram Content Group UK Ltd.
UKHW042239011124
450424UK00001BA/96

9 798227 436306